"Robbie Whelan's novel, *Lisa Is Not A Slut*, is a compelling, suspenseful, psychologically descriptive work. Reading and journeying with Lisa from the time she first hears "a voice," through the ever increasing tension of "auditory hallucinations" I was intensely focused on Lisa, Robbie's main, ever so real, character, and her desperate, deeper psychotic experience kept "invisible" from family and friends."

~ Rev. Dr. Cheryl A. Jones Cumbee, Clinical Consultant, Pastoral Psychotherapist and the Founding Executive Director of Faith Counseling Center, Scottsdale, Arizona

I0517007

LISA
is not A SLUT

A story by

Robbie Whelan

For my mother

Visitation

I was only sixteen when they came.

I remember it was on a Sunday. It was the usual Sunday, I guess. I went to church with the family, did some homework, watched The Simpsons cartoon with my sister and dad, then turned off the lights in my room and lay down to go to sleep around ten that night. I thought I was alone in my room. I had no idea that something unseen was about to announce its presence, instantly transforming my life upon its arrival.

It happened, they came, when I was at the edge of a dream, about to drift off to sleep, when I heard a voice say, "You forgot to pray." Startled, I sat up in bed and looked around my room. There was nothing. No one. Just my empty room. I began to get a little scared. Who had said that? "Hello?" I said. At first there was no response, but after a few seconds the voice I'd just heard spoke again, saying, "If you don't pray before you go to bed, if you die in your sleep, then you might not go to heaven."

I looked around my room and still saw no one. I thought maybe the voice came from someone in my closet. The door to it was closed. But who would be in my closet, and at that hour of the night? I wondered if it was my sister Samantha. She used to play jokes on me like this when we were both younger, but it didn't seem like something she would do now—that, and it didn't sound like her voice. Maybe she was disguising her voice. If so, she was talented at it, but I'd never heard her make different voices before.

"We're not Samantha," said the voice.

We? There was more than one person in my closet? I was totally shocked by how whoever was speaking seemed to know I'd been thinking they might be Samantha. It was like they'd read my mind. At that moment I was starting to get really frightened. I wanted to jump out of bed and run into my parents' room, but I was frozen. I kept telling myself to get up, but my body wouldn't listen. My imagination gushed with ideas about who was in my closet and what reason they had for hiding themselves in my room. I started thinking they might be intending to rape me. This thought finally sent me into action. I bolted from my room and ran down the hallway, through the living room, past the kitchen, and into my parent's room. They were out of it at first, still half asleep, and I had to tell them a few times why I had come into their room before what I was saying finally sunk in.

"Someone's in your room? Who?" my dad said.

"I don't know. They're hiding in the closet!"

"How do you know?" asked my mom.

"Maybe you just had a bad dream," my dad commented.

"I heard them. They talked to me."

"OK. Let's go check. Go back to bed, Margaret, I'll handle this," said my dad climbing his way out of bed.

When we got to the open door of my room, I grabbed my dad by the shoulder and told him to wait, that maybe he should get a weapon before he went in and checked my closet.

"A weapon?" he said. "We don't have any weapons in the house."

"What about one of your golf clubs?"

"Lisa, I think it will be OK. I think you might have just scared yourself into thinking someone was in your closet."

"Dad, I'm telling the truth. I told you I heard them. Please, Dad, get a golf club".

"Fine. OK." he said as he turned to walk to the garage where his golf bag was hanging. I didn't want to be left alone at the door of my room where the intruders were hiding, so I followed him. On the way to and back to my room from the garage, I thought some more about how the voice I'd heard seemed to have responded to what I'd been thinking about my sister. A rapist was one thing. That was realistic, but a regular human rapist couldn't read your mind. Had they really read my mind? I thought maybe it could have been a coincidence, but what were the odds that they would tell me they weren't Samantha right when I was wondering if they were? It made no sense. The more I thought about it, the more perplexed, and frightened I became.

When we got back to my room I told my dad that maybe we should call the police instead of going in. "What if they have a gun?" I said. My dad responded to this like he didn't think it was a good idea. I could tell that he still

3

didn't really believe there were people in my closet, but I grabbed him by the arm and persisted to tell him we should call 911 instead of confronting the intruders on our own. He finally gave in slightly, meeting me halfway.

"Go grab your mother's cell phone from the kitchen counter, then wait here in the hallway while I go in and check your room. If you hear me yell then run out of the house and call 911, but not until I yell. OK?"

Even though I still thought we should call the cops first, I went and got the cell phone and returned to the entrance of my room where my dad was waiting to go in with his golf club. Then from somewhere behind me in the dark of the hallway came my mother's voice, saying, "Bill, is everything OK? I got worried when you didn't come back to bed. "

"Everything's fine," my dad said to her.

"Just a bad dream then?" my mother asked.

"No," I said, "We haven't checked the closet yet."

"Is that golf club for protection? If there's someone really in the closet we should call 911. They might have a gun."

"That's what I said," I told my mom.

"No," my dad said, "We still don't know if there's anyone in there. I'm going to go check real quick. Lisa has your cell phone. I told her to run out of the house and call 911 if she hears me yell out after I check the room. You do the same, Margaret."

My mom started to get a worried look on her face. "Should I wake Samantha up, too?", she asked my dad.

"No. Let her sleep. It's probably nothing."

4

"Dad," I said, frustrated, "I heard them speak to me. I really did. They're in my closet. I know they are."

"I'm not running out of my house without both my daughters," my mom said.

"I agree, Mom," I said. "I'll go wake her up."

"Look. I'm done talking about it. I'm going in." My dad sank from view into the darkness of my room. I stopped in my tracks and waited.

"Lisa if there's anyone in there I'll run and get your sister and we'll meet you outside," said my mom in a comforting voice.

"OK," I said, hardly listening to her, concentrating more on what sounds, if any, were coming from my room, clutching the cell phone in my sweaty palm, ready to sprint my way to the front yard as soon as my dad gave the signal. When I heard my dad open my closet door, I waited in anxious anticipation for him to yell out, followed by sounds of a physical confrontation between my dad and the intruders. No such sounds came, just my dad calling from my room, "The closet's empty. No ones in here."

My mom rubbed my shoulder. "It was just a bad dream. A dark room can play tricks on your imagination."

My fear was a little bit less at that moment, but I was still scared because I was certain someone had been in my closet. I thought maybe they had ran out of the house while I was in my parents' room, or even scarier, maybe they were still somewhere in the house, in a new hiding spot, waiting until my parents went back to sleep, before they came into my room and did to me the awful things I imagined they were planning to.

While I was thinking about all this my mom tried to comfort me some more by massaging my back. As my dad reemerged from the darkness of my room into the hallway, I said, "I know there was someone in there. They talked to me. I heard them. They said 'we' like there was more than one of them."

"Well, I just checked your closet and there was no one in there. My job is done. I'm going back to bed," my dad said sounding tired.

"Wait," I protested. "They could still be in the house."

"I think we would have heard something," my mom said.

"I'm telling the truth. I heard them. I really did. Right when I was falling asleep they spoke to me. They talked about what I was thinking."

"It was probably the beginning of a bad dream that started and ended so quickly it felt like you were never asleep," said my dad.

I considered this. I had been about to fall asleep when I heard the voice. Maybe it was all just a dream, but it had seemed so real. I hoped my parents were right, I wanted to be the wrong one, but the fear I felt was stronger than this hope, and I couldn't shake the sense that I'd really heard someone in my room, which was accompanied by the suspicion that whoever it was who had spoken to me was still somewhere in the house hiding with their accomplice or accomplices.

"Can I sleep in your guys' room tonight?" I asked my parents.

"If you really feel you have to," my dad barely had finished saying before my mom contradicted his statement by saying, "No, Lisa. You're not a little girl anymore."

I turned towards my dad. "Please. Please. Please let me sleep in your room."

"It's your mother's decision," my dad said, glancing towards my mom as we both waited for her to respond.

My mom then said to my dad, "If we let her sleep with us tonight then she'll want to sleep with us tomorrow, and every other time she thinks she hears something in the night." Then she directed herself towards me, looking right at me. "You're going to be on your own in less than two years when you go off to college, and you're going to have to learn to deal with your fears on your own, because we're not going to be there to comfort you."

I felt like crying, but I didn't. I think I was as scared of the idea of being on my own as I was over there being intruders still hiding somewhere in the house waiting to commit a sex crime against me as soon as my parents left. After they went back to bed and I finally worked up enough courage to return to my room, I lay awake in bed, still too anxious to fall asleep, thinking about whether I'd really heard anything. I kept my eyes locked on my open closet, watching a swirl of shadows that appeared to be dancing there in the darkness, threatening to solidify into the shape of a person who wanted to do me harm. I nervously glanced back and forth from there to my bedroom entrance, waiting for someone to open it and come in, while I listened for sounds coming from outside my room that gave any indication that the intruders had emerged from their hiding spot and were making their way down the hallway towards my room. All the usual house noises, like the sound of the air-conditioner turning itself on and off, that I'd never really noticed before gained a newfound significance.

I don't know how long I waited there in the darkness before I allowed myself to fall asleep. When you're waiting for something you fear will happen any moment, something that never happens but always seems just about to, time passes by in a slow crawl, as every second becomes weighted down by anticipation. So, how much time had passed, I couldn't tell you. It could have been a half hour, or even a full hour, maybe more, until my fears began to calm, their power over me shrinking as my anxiety receded to the back of my mind, ebbing away until it was barely there. As these fears left I became less and less conscious of the house noises going on around me, until I finally allowed myself to close my eyes, feeling more and more at peace with my situation. Certain I was alone, with no one in my house but my family and me, I returned to the edge of a dream, just about to slip off into sleep, when I heard the voice again.

"You forgot to pray. You want to go to heaven, don't you? If you don't pray before you go to bed, if you die in your sleep, you might not go to heaven," said the voice, repeating what it had said before.

The words hit me like a bucketful of icy cold water, instantly jolting me awake in a single convulsive shiver that shook my whole body back into a state of full alertness as all my previous fears returned in amped intensity. I looked all around my room. No one. Nothing. There was nowhere for anyone to hide. Where had the voice come from? It sounded like it had come from the other side of my ceiling, from somewhere way up high. I frantically wondered if the people I'd thought had been in my closet were now up in the attic, or maybe even on the roof. This didn't make sense, nothing I was thinking did; how could they be looking into my room at me if we were separated by walls? I glanced up at the air-conditioning vent wondering if maybe they had installed a camera to spy on me. But why? This didn't make any sense. Who would do something like that? Who had spoken to me?

Who would be spying on me?

The idea of this seemed just as ridiculous as all the possible explanations I could come up with to explain what was happening. No one had ever described to me anything like what was happening to me, so I had to rely on things I'd read in books or seen on TV shows and in movies. I thought about 1984, that book by George Orwell I had to read in English, in which the government spies on everyone constantly with cameras placed everywhere. Why would the government want to spy on me, a sixteen-year-old girl? I mean, it's not like I was a terrorist or anything. I didn't do drugs or anything illegal. It didn't make sense. I thought about science fiction movies I'd seen where beings from another planet observed people from their spaceships and sometimes abducted people so they could perform experiments on them.

Were they space aliens?

Not in the attic, not on the roof, but somewhere high in the sky, speaking down to me from their spaceship? Were they going to take me up into it? As I thought about this, my cousin Jonathan popped into my mind, I guess because he's the only person I'd ever discussed aliens with. He was obsessed with shows like The X-Files, science fiction comic books, Star Trek, Star Wars, anything having to do with aliens or space travel. When we had our one and only alien conversation, he told me that getting abducted by space travelers from another planet was his biggest dream. He even said that he sometimes prayed to God asking Him to let this happen. I don't think I really believed in that kind of stuff. No one else I knew talked how my cousin did, so what he was saying seemed pretty weird to me. I didn't really have any opinions one way or the other towards the existence of space aliens, and I'd never even thought about it until my conversation with Jonathan. I don't even re-member how we got on the topic of space aliens, but I do remember asking him a few questions, just to contribute something to the conversation, like where he thought aliens came from and why they came to Earth. He said he thought aliens came from faraway places, other planets, and that he believed there were different kinds of aliens, some good ones that wanted to help the human race, and some bad ones who wanted to take over our planet and enslave us, "like angels and demons," he'd said.

The intensity with which Jonathan said all this put me on edge. I didn't like thinking about stuff like that. It made me feel strange. What if I thought about it and couldn't stop, until it became all I ever thought or talked about? All my friends would think I was weird and I would become an outcast in school the way Jonathan is, with no one to sit with at lunch except with all the geeky kids who played role playing games and stuff like that. I treated what Jonathan was saying like a contagious virus I didn't want to catch. I had wanted to move on to talk about something else and never think about it again; but right then, in my room, I was thinking about aliens again, thinking maybe I was hearing them talk to me from a spaceship hovering somewhere above my house.

Just thinking this made me frightened. It wasn't just the possibility that this odd theory could be true, it was also the idea of even thinking a thought like this in the first place. It filled me with panic. This thought seemed like a stranger to my other regular thoughts, which all seemed related to one another. All my normal thoughts all seemed to bubble up into my awareness from the same place, but these strange thoughts about aliens were so different from anything that I'd ever thought that they didn't even seem like my own thoughts. Like they'd come from somewhere other than my head. Alien. Yes, exactly, the thoughts I was having about aliens were to me like aliens themselves. They had abducted me into a bizarre state of mind, which was so unlike anything I'd ever experienced that it alienated me from myself.

It didn't feel like something I would think, but I was thinking it.

I didn't really believe in aliens, did I? But then what else could have said what I'd heard? Whoever, whatever, it was, had told me to pray. Pray? Why would space aliens want me to pray? What Jonathan had said about some aliens being like angels and others like demons came back to me. If the voice I'd heard had come from aliens, aliens that wanted me to pray, then this must've meant that they were good aliens, who were somehow working for God; and if they worked for God, I thought, then maybe they weren't aliens, but angels.

Angels! Now that was less scary to think about than aliens. Everyone close to me at that time believed in angels. My family was very religious: my older sister was married to a preacher who sometimes gave sermons at our church, we said grace before every meal, and the voice I'd just heard talking to me in my room had echoed what my mom had repeatedly told me from as early as I can remember—that I should always say my prayers before bed. To me, angels seemed more realistic than space aliens, and less odd to think about, I guess, because the only people I'd ever heard talk about aliens as if they were real were weird kids like my cousin Jonathan. Even my mother, who had been told the same thing by her mother, said that angels were real. Whenever there was a close call where something bad almost happened, like if we were in the car driving on the road when an accident with another car nearly happened, as soon as this potential disaster was avoided, my mom would always thank God, then say, "An angel must be watching over us today." She said that every time something bad didn't happen. I remember asking my mom about angels when I was a little girl. I asked her why I couldn't see angels if they were there. She told me they were invisible but they were there, always working to protect us and keep us on a righteous path towards heaven.

My mom told me that when you died you became an angel. I believed her. I believed everything my mom said when I was little. It was like she knew everything. After my grandmother died, my mom told me that she was up in heaven with the angels, always watching over me. I didn't doubt this for a second. If I ever thought about doing something bad, like taking a cookie from the cookie jar before dinner or something even worse than that, like cheating on my homework, even when no one was there to catch me and it seemed like I could get away with it, right when I was about to give in to the temptation, I always hesitated and thought about my grandmother. As far back as I could remember whenever I thought about doing something I knew was wrong I always felt the judging eyes of someone watching me, even when I was alone. This invisible presence had always remained mute; but, I wondered, was the voice I had just heard from one of these watchers looking down on me from heaven? Could it be possible? Did the voice come from someone on the other side? Not coming from rapists in my closet, or from spies in the attic or up on the roof, or from aliens in a spaceship above the Earth, but from angels in heaven. Was this true? Was I right?

"We're your angels," the voice said, confirming my thoughts. I was startled, in amazement. It couldn't have been a coincidence this time; the voice had definitely been in response to what I'd been thinking, as if the speaker had been following my train of thought just like it was reading words from a page in a book. It couldn't be a person. People can't see into your mind. It had to be something magical. The most magical thing I could think of was an angel. The voice had just said that's what it was, and I couldn't think of any reason not to believe what it said. It was so unbelievable, but I believed it. What else could I believe? How else could I make sense of this? Angels, I thought, angels, angels, angels! Was I dreaming? Could this really be happening? I wondered.

"Yes," said a voice different from the one that had spoken before, "we're here to make sure you don't go to hell."

Then the one who had spoken before said, "Pray," so I began to, silently in my head. As I thought this prayer to God a third voice different from the other two began repeating everything I was thinking. It was so bizarre, hearing my thoughts verbalized out loud as I thought them, by a voice that sounded like it was coming down through the ceiling from somewhere up in the sky. I didn't understand why the angel was mimicking my thoughts with its voice. As I wondered this, one of the angels responded, "He is telling your prayer to God." This just left me more puzzled. Wouldn't God hear my prayer without the need of an angel relaying the message to Him? I wondered. Didn't God hear everyone's prayers?

"We're God's messengers."

This made sense. I'd heard this said once before about angels, I think, in Sunday school. But I was left with more questions. How come I had never heard an angel say my prayer to God before? Had God heard those prayers?

"We were there. You just couldn't hear us."

I was satisfied by this answer. It was just like what my mom had told me when I was little about angels being there even though you couldn't see them. If what angels did was usually invisible to people, and they were there when they didn't seem to be there, then it made sense that what they said could also go unheard. I'd heard many stories from the Bible about people who had actually seen angels as well as heard them speak. An angel came to Mary and told her she was going to give birth to the Son of God. But that was Mary, the Holy Virgin, pure and without sin. I was just an ordinary girl, wasn't I? It must be up to God who hears angels and who doesn't. Why had God picked me?

I wanted answers to these questions. I started to ask when an angel repeated the word "Pray."

"What should I pray about?" I asked.

"Pray for your soul," said an angel. "The devil wants it."

This comment darkened somewhat the euphoric amazement the angels had begun to inspire in me. I had no longer thought I was in danger of being harmed by the speaker of the voice once I'd figured out it was coming from an angel, but once an angel brought up the devil, the boogeyman of the world, the most evil being in existence, it scared me to think that not only did he know who I was, but he also wanted my soul to be his.

I followed the angel's instructions and prayed for God to protect my soul and keep the devil away as an angel's voice echoed my thoughts in the background, telling my prayer to God. God. My creator. The creator of the universe. My voice was entering His ears right at that moment. I'd always heard in church that God listened to the prayers of everyone, but up until that moment God had seemed far away, out of touch, and now it felt like God was right there in my room, paying special attention to me.

Me. Why me?

This question was cut short by an angel reminding me to finish my prayer. I didn't know what to pray for next. "Pray for your family," an angel said. I did this, and then I came up on my own with a few things to pray about, hoping to impress the angels. When I ran out of ideas for what else to pray for I said, "Amen," as the echoing angel said it, too.

Then there was silence. I waited a few seconds for the angels to speak again, and then said, "Hello?" like I was asking the silence a question I expected to have answered. I received no response. They were gone. The angels were gone. To be sure of this I asked, "Angels, are you still there?" I received no reply, nothing, no sounds other than the hum of the air-conditioner vibrating through the house.

Now that everything seemed to be back to normal, I began to reflect on what had happened. Had I really spoken with angels? Could it all just have been a dream? The whole night just a dream? Was I still dreaming? I pinched myself just to make sure. The pain I felt where I pinched my arm felt as real as the angels' voices had sounded. Then I thought maybe I had just woken up and didn't know I'd been asleep. This was the same explanation my dad had given for why I'd believed I'd heard voices coming from my closet, but doubting that I'd just had a conversation with angels was doubting my own senses. I'd heard what I'd heard. It wasn't a dream. It was real, so, so real, I just knew it was. Angels were real. God was real.

Though I never dared tell anybody, I had sometimes secretly doubted the existence of God. If I ever told my mom this I was sure it would make her cry. I wanted to believe in God. I wanted what my parents believed in to be true. Almost every explanation they gave me in response to my childish wonder had something to do with God. Why? Because of God, because of God, because of God. If God wasn't real then everything my parents had taught me had been false. And if they were wrong, I didn't know what to believe. These hidden doubts about God felt chaotic in my head when I thought them, as if they were charged with an explosive energy that could blow up the entire world. I tried to ignore these thoughts. I knew you had to have faith in God. I'd heard it said many times before in church that God rewarded you for having faith, so I tried to have faith, but my faith seemed weaker than everyone else's in church. Other people didn't seem to have the same questions about God that I did.

But everything had changed after having angels come into my room. My biggest questions about God had been answered. All my nagging doubts had been replaced with an absolute certainty that God was real. I felt a strong sense of gratitude towards the angels for this. The angels, where had they gone? Back up to heaven, I supposed. I lay in bed for a few hours unable to fall asleep, all hyped up on an emotional cocktail of excitement mixed with edgy nervousness, while the conversation I'd had with the angels repeated itself over and over again in my thoughts.

What the angels had said about the devil wanting my soul stood out the most from all they'd said. This made me think of a nightmare I used to always have when I was little, where the devil came into my house and kidnapped me from my parents. Whenever I woke from this dream, I would walk into my parents room crying. My mother would tell me to crawl into bed with them where she'd hold me in her arms, rubbing the back of my head, which was facedown buried in her shoulder, as she whispered in my ear, "It's OK, baby, you're safe now. No one's going to hurt you. Mommy's got you. It was just a bad dream."

As I ruminated on this memory, I wondered if the devil from those long-ago nightmares was the same devil the angels had mentioned. Were those dreams real? I remember I would always wake up from those dreams feeling doomed. Doomed, such a heavy word, but that was the best way to describe how I felt. Doomed. Was I doomed? No, the angels had said they were there to make sure I didn't go to hell. That meant it was undetermined, it could go either way. In church I often heard the preacher say that God gave us the power to beat the devil when we put our faith in Him. This was what I was going to do. I would fight off the devil. At that moment I promised myself, and God, that I would devote myself to Him. From that point on I was going to be a better Christian. I wanted to live in service of Him. I even began to consider becoming a missionary when I grew up. I would spread His word to the hungry souls living in the most wretched parts of the world. That's how I would protect myself from the devil.

I don't know when I finally got to sleep. It might have been as late as three a.m. when I finally did. Maybe even later than that. But even with this lack of sleep, when my mom woke me up at six for school, I jumped out of bed right away, feeling fully energized, charged up with exuberant joy. This was out of the ordinary. Even when I'd had my regular hours of sleep my mom usually had to nag me out of bed. Most of the time it took three tries for her to get me moving to the breakfast table. The same scenario played itself out daily. After my mom woke me I would tell her "I'm up" just to get her to go away so I could fall back to sleep, and I would keep doing this every time she returned to my room to wake me, until finally she would begin to physically pull me out of bed by the arm as I said, "I'm up, I'm up." When my mom saw me jump out of bed the first time she came in, she looked at me surprised, and said, "Who are you and what have you done with my daughter?"

At breakfast I wanted to tell my mom about the angels, but I didn't know how to, and I was sure she would have told me it was all just a dream. Then again, maybe not, she did believe in angels. Still I didn't think she would have believed that her daughter was capable of hearing them. I probably wouldn't have believed me either if I were her, so I kept silent about it.

When I'd just about finished my bowl of cereal, my mom sat down at the table with me and said, "So, I'm glad to see my daughter still alive and in one piece. We had quite a scare last night, didn't we? Your dad must have scared those criminals away with his golf club."

What my mom said annoyed me. Showing my annoyance towards her in my voice, I responded, "There wasn't anyone in my closet, OK? I know that now, so just drop it."

"Your mother is just teasing you, honey."

"I know. I don't think it's funny."

"All right, all right, honey. So it was all just a bad dream then?"

"No, it wasn't a dream."

"Then what was it?"

The best response I could come up with was " I don't know," and when my mother pressed for more information I told her I didn't want to talk about it anymore, and thankfully this made her back off. If I went into any more detail I would have had to admit to my mother that the voices I'd thought had been coming from a rapist in my closet had really come from angels up in heaven. Saying this would worry her. I knew my mother thrived on routine. Anything out of the ordinary made her anxious.

But I felt bad about telling my mother I didn't know what I'd heard because it was a lie. I did know. I'd heard the angels, and even though I couldn't hear them at that moment, I was certain they were looking down on me, which meant they had witnessed me lie. The disappointment I felt towards myself was what I imagined the angels must also feel about me lying. The day had only just begun and I had already broken my promise to be a better Christian. This feeling didn't last long, though, and the extreme happiness I had felt when I first woke up returned by the time I was done eating. I had never felt so good. I wondered if this feeling was a gift from the angels. Was this what it felt like to become saved? The people in church who talked all the time about being saved seemed perpetually happy and full of energy.

Was this how I was going to be from now on?

I wanted to make up my lie to my mother, so before I went to take a shower, I told her I thought I was saved. My mom seemed happy to hear this; she wanted to hear more, and I wanted to say more, but I had to be careful not to tell her everything, while at the same time not telling her a lie. Tiptoeing across this tightrope, I said, "You know how scared I was last night after I thought there were people in my closet, right? Well, after you guys went back to bed I lay awake still worried that the people were hiding somewhere else in the house waiting to come out and get me. Something convinced me to pray to God, and I asked Him to keep me safe, and it felt like God was really there, listening to me, and my fears began to go away, and I began to feel real peaceful."

It was the most I had talked to my mother in a single sitting in a long time. She was always trying to get me to talk. I thought she would be blown away, but all she said in response was "I am so happy to hear you say that" without enthusiasm, in the same tone of voice she'd used the night before when she'd told me I'd just had a bad dream. Even though she didn't say this about my story, that's what I heard her say: It was just a dream. Feeling defensive, I said, "Mom. I'm telling the truth. It really happened."

"Don't be so sensitive, Lisa. I believe you, honey. What reason do I have not to?"

"You don't sound like you do."

"Well, Momma's still a little tired and is waiting for her first cup of coffee to kick in," she said

"OK. I guess I forgive you," I said, as if I were making a joke of the whole thing. But I was serious. God would have wanted me to forgive her.

He was watching me.

I now knew; God, and His angels, were always watching me.

Something Amazing

On the bus ride to school that morning I was more talkative than usual. Two of my closest friends, Julie and Stephanie, whom I knew from church, rode on the bus with me, and the two of them were jabbermouths, especially Julie. Most of the time I would sit back quietly listening to them talk back and forth. That's what people said, I was quiet. I guess I'd always been that way. I often wished I were more talkative, but I never knew what to say. It was like other girls like Julie and Stephanie had a constantly flowing word faucet in their heads that I lacked. My mom said I was just shy. She said I'd been that way ever since I was just a baby. But I wasn't feeling shy that morning on the bus. I don't know what it was, but I just talked and talked and talked. It was like I was someone else, spitting out words as if possessed by a foreign spirit that had taken over my speech faculties. I wasn't even sure I was making sense. I was just talking about whatever popped into my mind, excluding one subject, the one thing I really wanted to talk about but was afraid to share with my friends: the angels.

My sudden verbal explosion didn't go unnoticed by my two friends.

Julie said, "Boy, you're especially giddy this morning. I've never heard you talk so much. Slow down. You're making me dizzy."

Stephanie agreed with Julie. "Yeah, you're super hyper today." Stephanie always agreed with Julie, it seemed; Julie, who then said, "What, did you drink like ten Red Bulls?"

"No. I can't help it, I just feel high right now, but it's all natural."

"What do you know about what being high feels like? You've never done a drug in your life. You wouldn't even take a sip of the wine cooler I smuggled out of my house that one night at Steph's, little Miss Goody Two Shoes."

"OK. I feel like how I imagine being high must feel."

"How come?" asked Stephanie.

Without thinking I blurted out, "Something amazing happened last night," and as the words left my mouth I heard someone shush me from the seat one row behind mine. In search of the source of this shushing noise, in one quick motion, I lifted myself up and jerked my body around, placing my knees where my butt had been as I turned my body facing to the back of the bus. Once I had worked myself into this position, I looked down at the seat behind mine at a kid named Tommy. Tommy never said anything. He wasn't just shy like me, he was socially awkward, big time. He always looked nervous, his face got bright red in class when the teacher called on him to talk, and all his facial muscles would flex and unflex in an expression that was a cross between how someone looked while in deep concentration and how they looked while taking a massive poop. I know that's mean, but I'm serious, that's what he looked like. When he finally talked he panted loudly between every other syllable as if he were out of breath from running laps around a track. That was Tommy in a nutshell, but none of this explained why he would shush me. It didn't seem like something he'd do. He didn't talk unless spoken to. But if he didn't shush me, then who? All the seats behind him were empty. Not that many kids rode our bus. There was just like ten of us.

"Hello...Earth to Lisa," said Julie.

Stephanie let out a small giggle and said, "What is she doing"?

"I don't know," responded Julie. "She's totally bonkers today."

I was still looking down at Tommy, who was now staring up at me with a painful expression, his eyes all twitchy, like looking at me hurt him, as if he were gazing directly into the sun.

I gave him a big smile and giggled through my teeth. "Hi," I said.

"Um...uh...hi," he said as if he were sure he was giving the wrong answer to a question.

I continued to giggle while looking down at him with a wild grin that must have made me look like a crazed lunatic. I don't know why I was behaving this way towards him. I feel bad about it now; thinking back, it's obvious he was really sensitive and probably thought I was laughing at him. But I wasn't laughing at him. At least I don't think so. I don't really know what I was laughing at. I just found the whole situation absurdly funny for some reason.

I realized I knew nothing about him other than that he looked like he was taking a poop when he talked. All of a sudden I became curious towards him. I'd never really interacted with him before, and out of nowhere I felt a strong desire to interrogate him with a million questions.

"How are you?" I said.

"Uh...I'm fine."

I continued to grin at him like the Joker from Batman. I tried to make eye contact with him, but the second we locked stares he broke away, glancing from my eyes to my nose, then down at my maniac smile. It was aggressive, trying to look him in the eyes, like an attack. I felt like I was playing a part in a movie. I pictured an imaginary audience laughing hysterically at my performance. They got the joke.

"Aren't you going to ask me how I'm doing?"

"How...how...are you?"

"I'm fantastic, Tommy," I said, then paused for a moment, waiting to read my next line from the movie script, which was, "Are you surprised I know your name, Tommy?"

"I...um...don't know," he said.

"Because I've had, like, four classes with you. I bet you don't know my name, though, do you?"

"Yes...I do...," he said, exasperated.

"Then what is it?"

"It's...it's...um...," he began saying. I could tell he was drawing a blank. He probably knew my name but had temporarily forgotten it because of how nervous I was making him.

"It's Lisa. I can't believe you didn't know!" I said in my best hurt-actress voice.

"I knew that."

"Then why didn't you say it?"

"I was going to."

I was about to continue this belittling line of questioning when all of a sudden I began to feel guilty, like I was doing something wrong. The intoxicated feeling, which had elevated me into a euphoric state of ecstasy—a powerful sensation that had been present at the start of my conversation with Tommy—abruptly abandoned my senses without warning, leaving me sober, with a changed perspective. I was no longer the actor spouting out lines I'd memorized from a script, but was sitting in the invisible audience that had been viewing this scene. I felt what the audience felt. The joke had gone too far. The character I'd been playing began to seem like a cruel villain torturing Tommy, the poor, helpless victim. I knew it was just a pretend audience I'd made up, and that this wasn't really a movie, it was real life, but thinking about this made me think of the real, not pretend, audience that was actually watching this—and I'm not talking about Julie and Stephanie, I'm talking about the angels, and God, looking down from heaven in judgment of how I was behaving. In one moment I had gone from feeling dopey and silly to feeling serious and self-critical. I was not acting like a Christian towards Tommy. I shouldn't have been having fun at his expense. A person with a true faith in Jesus would reach out to Tommy with compassion and attempt to soothe his social anxiety by offering him the complete and loving acceptance of Jesus Christ. What would Jesus do? He certainly wouldn't make funny faces at Tommy. I wanted to turn all this around and treat Tommy like Christ would have. I could feel the unseen presence of the angels, who were observing all this, and I wanted to make them proud of me.

So, I was cast in a new role, the part of Jesus, but I couldn't remember the lines from the script. What would Jesus say? I gave my best impression of Christ, and said, "Tommy, you should know, God loves you." My words sounded superficial to my ears. I was sure Jesus would have come up with something cleverer to say. Even so, based on the way Tommy was looking at me right then, it was evident I'd made a sizeable impression on him. He looked completely flabbergasted, wide-eyed, jaw dropped, his mouth gaping open, as if I had just given him the most shocking news of his life.

"It's true, Tommy. And, if you put your faith in the Lord, He will make the devil leave you, and you won't get nervous when you talk anymore. Words will flow out of your mouth with ease. When you let God into your heart, He will take away all your fear. The devil won't be able to touch you. You'll be protected. His angels will watch over you and guide you towards righteousness. And when you read the Bible and follow His word, it will lead you down the path to everlasting life in heaven. Doesn't that sound good?"

"Um, yeah."

My jubilation from before was returning. I was so proud of myself. I was sure the angels were, too. I was preaching the word of the Lord. I wasn't really aware of it at the time, but in retrospect, I was guilty of the sin of pride, because I felt a sense of superiority towards Tommy, as if the salvation of his soul depended on me. Like he was the sheep, and I, the shepherd.

I continued to preach the word of God to him, giving my best impersonation of church authority figures I'd often observed preaching about salvation, asking Tommy, "Have you accepted Jesus Christ into your life?"

"Do you mean, like, do I, like, believe in him?" he asked.

"Well, do you?" I asked.

"I believe in God," Tommy answered.

"I am so happy to hear you say that," I said, smiling down at him warmly, and not with the cheek-to-cheek wide-mouthed grin I'd given him at the beginning of our exchange, before this turned into a serious conversation about the Lord.

I felt holy and like I was shining all over; there was a warm, fuzzy feeling at the top of my skull, where I envisioned a golden halo ringed around my head, giving off a radiant glow. There was a new script now. The Bible. The lines were coming back to me. I was just about to read one off to Tommy from memory when Julie interrupted me.

"Lisa! Turn around! What's up with you today?"

"OK, OK," I said looking back at her. But before I sat back down and faced towards the front, I looked down at Tommy one last time and said, "Well, will you think about what I said?"

"Yes," he answered.

"If you have any problems, anything at all, come to me, and I'll pray with you. God will hear us. I know for a fact He will. Does that sound good?"

Before Tommy had a chance to respond, Julie broke into the conversation again, almost shouting: "Lisa!"

I turned back around to face her and in a full shouting voice, I screamed, "What do you want?" Some of the kids in the front of the bus turned around and looked at us, and I caught a glimpse of the bus driver's face in the rearview mirror glancing back in our direction. Both Julie and Stephanie looked blown away. I think I was just as surprised than they were, if not more. I couldn't remember the last time I'd shouted anything. I was sure it was the loudest noise that had ever come out of my mouth. I never ever raised my voice to anyone, and this sudden change of character added to the bizarre sense I had begun to develop before that I was playing a part in a movie.

"Oh my God! You don't have to shout. I'm worried about you."

"You shouldn't be. I got God watching my back, so I'm fine."

"Why were you talking to Tommy? Do you have a crush on him?" Julie asked, loud enough for Tommy to hear. I'm guessing she did that on purpose, to embarrass me, because she was annoyed by how I was acting. Usually something like that would really embarrass me, but it didn't have any effect on me that morning for some reason. However, I could almost feel Tommy's embarrassment coming from behind me.

"No. It's nothing like that. Hey, um, did you hear someone shush me a minute ago?"

"Shush you?" Julie said. "I didn't hear anything."

Looking towards Stephanie, I asked, "Did you?" and she shook her head no.

"Someone shushed me, but I don't know who."

"Neither of us heard anything," said Julie. "Are you sure you're OK?"

"I feel great," I said.

"I can tell," she said back.

"Lisa," said Stephanie, speaking up, "what was so amazing?"

"What?" I asked.

"You were about to tell us something before you turned around. You said something amazing happened."

I wanted to unload it all on them, tell them all about my conversation with the angels the night before; but I knew they would respond with disbelief, so even though the urge to tell them was so strong, I decided against it. I had to say something though. But what? I was at a loss for words. Suddenly life was real again, with no script to follow. Having no idea what to say, I began to speak anyway, saying, "Well. Um. It was something totally unbelievable. I can't really tell you guys. I'm sorry. I shouldn't have said anything in the first place."

"Why not?" asked Stephanie.

"Is it about a guy?" asked Julie.

This just made me smile for some reason.

"It so is. I can tell. Look how she's smiling. Who is it?" interrogated Julie.

"Nobody," I said.

"Come on," persisted Julie. "Tell us which guy. Is it Patrick? I know you like him. It's him, isn't it?"

"What? No! It's not about a guy. I promise."

"Then what was so amazing?" Julie asked.

"Nothing. I made it all up, OK?" I said without thinking, walking blindly headfirst into a sin. I'd told a lie again, forgetting for a moment, just like I had before at breakfast with my mom, the promise I had made to God the night before. The euphoric glow departed instantly as I started to get down on myself for committing yet another sin. And what Julie said next in response to my fib made me feel ten times worse. She started to sing a song I'd heard sung hundreds of times in church youth group: "Revelations, Revelations, burn, burn, burn, liars go to hell, liars go to hell, burn, burn, burn! Burn, burn, burn!"

I did not need to hear that right then. Up until that moment this jingle had always sounded lighthearted to me, I guess, because it was so singsong-y, and I had never really thought about the meaning of its words until right then. Hearing the song now, really, truly hearing it so the implications of every line sank in deep, filled me with a sense of dread and got my mind focused back on the devil again. It was as if hearing this song had reverted me back to being a little girl, and I had just had one of my nightmares about the devil kidnapping me from my parents' house, waking up feeling doomed. Doomed. There was that word again. Doomed. No, I'm not doomed, I thought, but the devil wanted my soul, the angels had said so, which meant I was in some kind of danger. But if I followed their instructions, I hoped, my soul would remain safe, and the devil wouldn't be able to get it.

Right?

I wanted to know for sure. I wished the angels were there right then to answer my questions. There was so much more I wanted to learn from them. I called out to them with my thoughts, thoughts they could somehow see me think, but I received no reply.

Would they ever return?

I was quiet for the rest of the bus ride as I pondered this. While I sat and thought, I looked out the window, and what I saw somehow began to lift my spirits and eventually broke my mind free from the grip of my dreadful thoughts about the devil. What I was seeing out the bus window put me in a state of awe filled wonder. I had never realized how beautiful everything was. Everything seemed more vivid and colorful than I remembered it being. The light of the morning sun seemed to be hitting everything just right. The green of trees and grass seemed greener; the blue of the sky, bluer; the sun, sunnier; the clouds, more fluffy and white; all the colors of life, brighter. It was like everything was alive and talking to me in a silent language I could hear with my eyes. I began to feel that God was communicating to me somehow through what I was seeing, making His presence known to me through the wondrous beauty of His creation, this world, this universe, everything that was and will be.

The incredible joy had returned.

It seemed to be coming into my body from outside.

Beaming down to me from heaven.

A lady we passed by was out watering her lawn, looking up into the sky at something, gazing heavenward, reminding me that as long as I remained faithful to Him, I would be OK.

Prophet

The sense of serenity that had come to me from looking out the window on the bus ride to school stayed with me the rest of the day. All day I daydreamed about the angels, thinking over and over again, "It happened, it really happened." My classes seemed to fly by and school was over before I knew it. I looked forward to my bedtime with anticipation, hoping that the angels would return again to converse with me and answer my countless questions.

I went to bed an hour early that night. My mom noticed this when I said good night and asked me if I was tired. The easiest thing would be to say yes, but I wasn't that tired and I didn't want to tell another lie, so I just acted like I didn't hear her, which, I guess, was a silent sort of lie. I thought about this walking into my room feeling a tinge of guilt. How hard it was not to sin! As I lay down to bed, I decided it was better to act like you didn't hear somebody than tell them a lie, so I had chosen the lesser of the two evils, which made me feel a little better.

I didn't want the angels to have to remind me to say my prayers, so I began to talk to God in my head while I waited for them to come back. I remembered to pray about all the things the angels had instructed me to pray about the night before, asking God to protect me from the devil and to watch over my family; then, after saying amen, I lay awake in bed, staring up at the ceiling, listening closely for the voices of angels. An hour of boredom passed without a word from an angel. It was a big letdown. Thirty minutes more went by, and still no angels. I finally began to get sleepy and shut my eyes, falling asleep, feeling disappointed.

Tuesday came and went with no visit from the angels, and Wednesday was just the same. On both these nights besides praying for what the angels had instructed me to on the night they appeared, I also prayed to God to send the angels back to me. It made me feel a bit like my cousin Jonathan praying to God to let him get abducted by space aliens—but this was different, I told myself. Space aliens probably didn't exist, but angels were definitely real. I knew they were, I'd had an actual conversation with them. I had, hadn't I? This question began to ask itself with increasing frequency as the time I'd spent with the angels drifted farther and farther into the past. By Thursday I was beginning to become partially convinced that it had all just been a dream, but there was still a part of me, a large part, totally convinced that what I'd experienced had been really real.

All day Thursday during school I prayed over and over again to God to bring the angels back. Being wrapped up in my thoughts like this, in constant silent prayer, I must have appeared more withdrawn than usual because my

English teacher took me aside before lunch and asked me if I was OK. I wasn't feeling good. I was feeling abandoned. I didn't want to tell my teacher this because it would make her ask more questions I also didn't want to answer, and I didn't want to lie either, so instead of giving her an answer, I just asked, "Why?"

"I ask," she said, "because you seem more distracted than usual. I asked you a question in class about the video we watched and then I had to ask it again because you weren't paying attention. Then you couldn't answer me, because you hadn't been paying attention to the video either. That's so unlike you. You're one of my best students. Is something on your mind?"

I was stuck. There was only two ways out, telling her a lie by saying nothing was on my mind—committing another sin—or I had to give her some kind of truthful answer. I was so anxious of what she might ask next that I couldn't lie, so I said, "Well, yes, there is something on my mind. I've been praying to God all day asking Him for something I really, really want."

My teacher seemed a bit surprised by this. "Oh," she said. "Well, I hope your prayers are answered," and then she let me go to lunch. I felt so relieved that she didn't ask more questions. Looking back I think she probably didn't ask anything else because teachers in public schools aren't supposed to discuss religion with their students; they can be fired for it, so I guess I lucked out.

Even though I was relieved walking to lunch, I was also a bit confused over why my teacher had said I seemed distracted. Was it really that obvious? Was it written on my face? I usually participated more in class, and even though

I was a naturally quiet person, I was also a straight-A student. I wanted a good participation grade, so I would force myself to speak up in class.

At lunch I continued to repeat my prayer in my head while I ate while Steph and Julie talked about I don't remember what. I was pulled out of my mind when I heard Julie say my name. I looked up at her as she asked, "What's wrong?"

"Nothing," I said.

" You look sad," she persisted.

"Well, I'm not. I feel fine. I just have a lot on my mind."

"Like what?" she asked.

"Just stuff."

"That's specific," she said sarcastically.

"I'll tell you about it later. Maybe," I said as I got up from the lunch table with my tray of food. "I'm going to the library to study for my math quiz next period." I had studied the night before, and I didn't need to study anymore, but I needed a reason to get away so I could be alone with my thoughts: my one long prayer to God asking Him to send the angels back to me. But I did go to the library and study a little just to make what I'd said to Steph and Julie not a lie. After going over a few problems, I dropped my pencil and continued praying. I thought if I prayed hard enough God would finally grant me my wish, but that night there was still nothing, no angels.

Then Friday came. I had finally given up on praying for the angels to return. I was expecting never to hear from them again, and I was beginning to think it might have been just a dream.

But I was wrong.

My constant prayer from the day before was finally answered.

I was in history class.

The period was almost halfway over, when I heard a voice say, "Pray." The moment I heard this I was flooded with bliss. The angels, I thought excitedly, they're back! The teacher was giving a lecture at the front of the room. Nobody else seemed to have heard anything. Why not? I wondered. "Only you can hear us," answered an angel, before saying, "Pray," once again. I did what the angel asked, thinking thoughts that instantly began to be carried up to heaven and into God's ears by the voice of an angel echoing my prayer. It was just as weird as the first time, hearing my thoughts broadcasted by a voice that wasn't mine, this time sounding like it was coming through the walls from another classroom. As I continued to pray I looked around the classroom for any sign that someone else heard what I was hearing. Nothing. So, it was true, nobody else could hear the angels. But, I wondered, why me? What made me so special? Why had God chosen me? I thought again about the select few people who could converse with angels that I'd read about in the Bible.

What was it about me that made me like them?

"You're a prophet," said an angel.

A prophet, I thought in question, I'm a prophet?

"You're a prophet," repeated the angel.

I'm a prophet, I thought.

Me, Lisa, a prophet.

What did this mean? My head flooded with questions. I wanted to ask the angels all of them, but as I began to an angel said, "Pray." Pray, I thought, I did pray. "You didn't finish," said the angel. What had I forgotten, I wondered. I'd prayed for God to keep the devil away and to protect my family; what else was there? Oh, that's right, I thought, I didn't say amen. This made me think of Sunday night when the angels first came. After I'd finished my prayer then, after I'd said amen, they had left without explanation.

I didn't want them to go yet.

Will you be back? I asked the angels in my thoughts.

"We'll be back," said one angel.

"Pray," said another.

Amen, I thought.

"Amen," repeated an angel.

Behind What They Saw

The angels did not come back for another week, but I did not despair because they had told me they would be back, and I believed them. They were angels, they couldn't lie; only the fallen angels could sin, and my angels came from heaven. I say my angels, but really they were God's angels, His messengers, sent down to tell me what He wanted me to hear.

That's what I believed.

During the whole week the angels were gone, I thought about them all the time. Even if they weren't there, they were there. They were silent, invisible, but I could feel their presence, feel their eyes watching me, and everything I consciously said and did I did because I thought it would make the angels, and God whom they served, happy with me. I evaluated all my actions the way I thought the angels would; what I thought the angels thought about what I was doing became what I thought about what I was doing. I was down on Earth with everyone else seeing life from the ground, but they, the angels, were far above the world where they saw everything. In my mind everything the angels thought was true. Their perception was divine, second only to God's. I wanted to see what they saw, but I couldn't, I could only guess. They didn't just see me from where they were, they could also see inside my head; my thoughts were visible to them. They knew me better than I knew myself, which meant what they thought about me was more true then what I thought about me; and because of this, what they thought was more important than what I thought, at least, more important to me: me, who was becoming in my mind not who I saw or who I thought other people saw but who I thought the angels saw. What I thought the angels thought became what I would think, and when I said something, like when I spoke to my mom or Steph and Julie or whoever, I said what I thought the angels wanted to hear me say, the Christian thing to say, what I thought the Lord Jesus Christ would say. It was like I was always talking to the angels no matter whom I was talking to; what the person in front of me heard and thought about what they heard became less and less of a concern. It was what the angels thought, and what God thought, that truly mattered.

Although, even though the angels were always in my thoughts, and even though I tried to act how I thought the angels wanted me to act, there were brief moments when I forgot about the angels, forgot they were watching me, and I would do or say something careless. I would sin, sin so fast, as fast as a thought is thought, sin in the blink of an eye, like I'd shut my eyes for a split second and the angels would be gone, and for that split second I would be blind, without my angel thoughts (what I thought the angels thought) to guide my actions. But the moment after I sinned, I would remember the angels, my eyes would blink open, and I would see what I had done and judge myself how I thought the angels were judging me up in heaven, and the angels' judgment was God's judgment. Afterwards I would try to make it up to God and the angels by going out of my way to behave in a Christlike way, which usually meant preaching to someone and trying to save their soul from damnation; I started talking about Jesus to everyone. People were beginning to notice this. My mom commented that I was becoming so spiritual lately, and she said she was happy to see it. Julie and Steph had made jokes about it, well, Julie did, but I consider everything Julie says to be something Stephanie would also have said, because Steph was always agreeing with Julie. If Steph said one thing and then Julie said the opposite, it would change Steph's mind; she would take back what she said and agree with Julie, almost always, as if Julie's perceptions were more valid than hers.

Julie was Steph's angel.

And that's how I used to be also, before the angels—well, not as bad as Steph, but I remember when what Julie thought about me was the most important thing in the world. How I thought she saw me shaped how I saw me. What she thought was cool was cool, she defined almost everything for me, what she said was contagious, it would get inside my head and repeat over and over until it became what I thought. It was almost mystical the way Julie influenced my perceptions. A boy would be just a boy, a boy like all the others, but then if Julie said he was cute, suddenly I would become attracted to him, and if Julie fell in love with him, so would I. I remember she was the first out of the three of us to like boys. I didn't like boys, not most of them; I found the majority of the boys in our class obnoxious and I didn't care what they thought, but when Julie started having crushes, boys suddenly mattered. Like magic, I started having crushes, too, and I began wanting boys to think about me what Julie wanted them to think about her: to think I was pretty. And strangest of all, almost the day after Julie sprouted breasts, so did I, as if my biological clock were timed to hers, but always a minute behind, because Julie had to be first, she always was.

But she wasn't the first to hear angels.

It's funny, the power other people can sometimes have over you, the way a certain person can get inside your head and change how you think and feel, as if your feelings flow from them into you, and as if your thoughts are thought from their head into yours; how you can suddenly see what they see when they tell you what they see, as if their words are sponges soaked in their reality that squeeze out into your mind when you hear them.

The point is that the angels were my new Julie. They were changing what I thought about everything. In one night I had gone from being an ordinary girl to a girl who heard angels, and then just a few days later I became a prophet. What did this mean? What made me a prophet? I didn't know, but the angels did, and I was waiting for them to come back and tell me why; waiting for them to redefine me again. My self-image had been completely transformed by them, and who I'd been before in my head became obsolete the moment an angel's voice entered my ears, as if their voices carried a new "me" into my head and now this new me was growing up. Who I was becoming was born that night, and on the day I found out from the angels that I was a prophet this new me took its first steps, and now the new me was waiting to go through puberty, when it, when I, would learn what it meant to be a prophet and what I was supposed to do for God. It was like I was waiting for Julie to tell me it was OK to grow breasts again as I waited for the angels to return and fill me with their knowledge.

I was a prophet. Me, Lisa, the girl who attended Ronald Reagan High School, the quiet girl in class everyone thought they knew. But who they thought they knew was not who I was; I was a prophet of God, I wanted to tell everyone. But I still saw who I'd been less than two weeks ago in their heads, I saw this in how they talked to me like I was someone like them, someone who didn't hear angels, who wasn't a prophet. I knew the second I told one of them I was a prophet who heard angels, the little me in their heads would be obliterated, and what they would think about me next would take the place of the old me. I didn't know what this person looked like, and I was scared to find out. They probably wouldn't believe me. They would laugh at me, call me crazy, and persecute me like they persecuted all the prophets in the Bible.

Was this what was supposed to happen? Did it come with the territory of being a prophet? I didn't think I was strong enough. I cared what people thought too much; but then again, I cared even more about what God thought, and if He believed I could handle being a prophet then it must be true. But I wasn't ready. Not yet.

The old me was a safe place to hide behind while I waited for the angels to tell me what to do, to tell me what a prophet did. I told myself as I thought about the angels, in school, at home, everywhere, that I would do whatever the angels asked me to, because their way was the way to heaven, to glory, and if I did what they said, the devil would be powerless. The devil? Who was he? When I heard people say "the devil" It would make me see a red-skinned man with sharp fangs, horns on his head, and the legs of a beast. This was a cartoon, that's how it was starting to seem, and the devil was no cartoon, he was real, I knew he was real. Ever since the angels had told me he wanted my soul I had been thinking about him a lot, almost as much as I thought about the angels; and as I did the red-faced devil of the movies was fading and a dark, shadowy, unformed figure with features I couldn't quite make out had taken its place: a boogeyman in the closet that could be anything, my worst fear waiting to be realized. This image of the devil was even scarier because it was filled with infinite possibility. It was undefined waiting to be defined, it was something that wasn't quite something, not yet, that was in the stage of becoming, with the potential for becoming anything, for assuming any form. The devil in my head was whatever I imagined him to be; the most awful, evil-filled entity I could come up with; a shape-shifting terror; fear personified.

Have you ever thought about someone so strongly it almost feels like they are there? That's how the devil was beginning to feel to me even though he was only a vague idea in my head. He wasn't there like the angels—I didn't feel him watching me like I felt the angels watching me, not yet, the devil still felt faraway, down in his hell, away from me—but every time I thought about him I felt him getting closer, as if I were thinking him to me. And the frequency with which I thought of him was increasing every day; the devil was bad weather coming my way, and the louder the thunder, the closer the storm. My thoughts were the thunder, and the devil was the storm. He was coming for me, I just knew. I felt it in my bones like arthritis. It was my nightmare on the verge of coming true.

But I had God and the angels on my side. I had to remember that, it was my protection, my safety net. I began repeating scripture in my head like a mantra to fight off the devil thoughts, as if holy thoughts were an antidote that pushed the devil back down into hell. I told myself, "Although I walk in the shadow of the valley of death I will fear no evil for the Lord is with me." The devil was the shadow and death and the Lord was sunshine and salvation. After I repeated the scripture in my thoughts long enough, eventually the words seemed to dissolve into a light that filled up my mind, the dark thoughts about the devil scattered like cockroaches into hiding, and it felt like God was right there with me. When I felt God with me, my head was full of light, my whole body full of pure, white light. I wanted to feel it all the time. It was my heroine, a taste of heaven.

This was a bit complicated in my mind, and hard to put into words. It had to do with who I was—who I was on the surface, who my friends and family knew, and who I was where they couldn't see, the parts of myself I kept hidden inside and would never show anyone because of how I thought revealing this side to others would change how they thought about me. That was where I was keeping the angels, this place inside. This other Lisa, the one no one saw, kept all my secrets for me. I say the other Lisa because hiding aspects of myself from other people made me feel like two people. I was who I saw reflecting back at me in their eyes, and I was who I was where their eyes could not see. Half of me was in the light with other people, and my other half lived in the shadows.

The light shone from their eyes, from the eyes of everyone.

I was frightened of this person within. What she wanted seemed destructive. It was she, and not the Lisa who lived in the light, who had doubted God before, and it was she who wanted to do things the Lisa everyone knew me as would never do. This other person sharing my body with me thought about sex and wanted to do it before marriage. She was curious about drugs and alcohol. She thought everything I would never say. She was everything in me not good. She was my sin, a black stain on my soul. At the times I forgot about the angels, when I had sinned, it was she who sinned; she would emerge from the dark depths within me, where I kept her pushed down, up into the light where she would become me for a moment, a moment of sin. After the sin was committed she would sink back into the shadows as I returned to myself in a wave of guilt.

My greatest fear was that I would one day become her.

But I was able to pretend she didn't exist most of the time. Like I explained earlier, who I thought I was in other people's minds was a mirror in mine where I saw myself, who I usually believed I was, but always in the back of my mind I knew what I saw in this reflection was incomplete, as if the Lisa I kept hidden was whispering from behind the mirror, whispering from the darkness into the light, "I exist. I am you." But I wasn't her. Not to my mom or my dad, my younger and older sisters, Steph and Julie, or all the people at school and everyone at the church. What everyone thought (or appeared to) had a powerful influence over me. What I thought everyone saw seemed like reality to me, and anything I saw that they didn't see seemed like a dream. I wanted some of my dreams to come true, to become what everyone saw, but I also had nightmares, and these nightmares would push up against the edge of reality, threatening to exist. But the angels had changed all this. Reality was no longer what I thought everyone else thought; reality had shifted to what I thought the angels thought. I was the only one who could hear them, but I was sure they were real and that what they said was also real. I was a prophet. The angels thought this; I thought it, too, but no one else did. They didn't know, but I did.

What I thought everyone else thought was turning into a dream.

I was becoming who they didn't see.

The light was inside now where the angels could see. But she was still in the darkness, my nightmare, the sinner; the light had not reached her yet, and I didn't want it to, I didn't want the angels to see her, because if they saw her, that's who I would be.

I was who they could see.

The Seduction

I didn't think a prophet should play with her vagina.

If she had one she left it alone. I was a good girl. A Christian. Everyone knew this. I was committed to saving myself for marriage, but I was a human, and thoughts about sex would sometimes enter my mind, usually to be ignored and swatted away like flies. But sometimes, not very often, like once or twice a month, late at night alone in my room I would finger myself and rub on my clitoris while I fantasized about sex until I brought myself to orgasm. The pleasure of every orgasm ended in guilt; the two sensations were attached at the hip, the last one staying with me the longest. The orgasm would only last for a few seconds, but the guilt could drag on for hours and even present itself the next day, when I would remember I masturbated: a sinner in the eyes of God. I had failed as a Christian. Remembering made me feel dirty. Gross. Sex was something you did with your husband after you were married. He was the one who was supposed to give you an orgasm; it wasn't something you were supposed to give yourself. I thought only bad girls did that. I was sure Julie and Steph never did it.

And I couldn't imagine my mom ever having touched herself the way I did.

One of my biggest fears was that she would find out. I would see her in my thoughts walking into my room the moment the orgasm came. This fear was soaked in pure shame, a poisonous thought that would split open in my head and spill its poison into my body. The only way to keep this from happening, to keep my mom from discovering I masturbated, was to stop masturbating; and in the guilt-drenched moments after I had done it, I would always make a promise to myself never to do it again.

Never again. Never again. Never again.

But the dark desire would eventually return and stay for days until I satisfied it. This urge felt like it came from somewhere outside my body, from I don't know where, and the temptation to sin would not go until sin was committed. I felt it in me like a living presence, a sin alive with determination, willing itself from thought to action; a nagging itch begging to be scratched.

The itch returned a day or so after I'd learned I was a prophet.

But that wasn't something I did, I told myself. Not anymore. That was in my past. I was someone else now, but the itch remained where it was, an attention-grabbing obsession ping-ponging between my angel thoughts and devil thoughts, a constant battle: what I didn't want to do that I wanted to do.

It was a weak moment. I did it.

I had forgotten about the angels for just a short time. It had been days since they'd come. They were gone, and the temptation was not. I was thinking about Patrick while in bed. He was a boy from my school who sat two rows across from me in English. We had only spoken a few times. I didn't think he thought of me the way I thought of him. When I stared at him in class I felt like something that didn't exist staring at something that did. Whenever he turned his head in my direction while I was looking at him, I would quickly look away, wanting to disappear. But I wanted him to notice me. I wanted to be someone he thought about. I wanted to be who he wanted.

I didn't know what Patrick looked like without clothes on. I filled in the blanks with bits and pieces cut from my memory where images from the one porno I had ever seen in my life were deeply buried like lava trapped in a dormant volcano I was digging a tunnel to.

My vagina was moistening. Calling out to be touched.

I slid two fingers between the slick, wet lips of my vagina and parted them while I pulled back the hood over my clitoris with my other hand. When the air lightly touched my exposed clit, it tingled with sensitivity, and when I finally touched it a powerful sensation that I felt with my whole body erupted as I let out a small, quiet gasp while Patrick in my head whispered into my ear how pretty he thought I was. He was touching me in my fantasy where I was touching me for real. We started to do some of the things I'd seen the people do in the porno movie. Not all the things. Not the real dirty stuff. Just normal sex things.

Patrick penetrated me with his penis from a porno movie. This image was surrounded by an invisible aura of guilt that would linger in the image's afterglow long after it had served its purpose; what I was seeing in my mind disgusted me even as it made my vagina moisten.

"I love you," Patrick said in my fantasy. "I will always love you, forever and ever."

Patrick was my husband. That's what I told myself in the fantasy. It made what we were doing not a sin, and it dammed up the guilt where it would remain until the fantasy was over.

"I want you to be the mother of my child," Patrick told me.

He was treating me so gently, kissing me softly, thrusting into me slowly, taking his time. I wanted this to last. I liked the way he was having sex with me, because I thought it was how married people did it. But I wanted him to do the other things, the awful, nasty things I had seen in the porno. The men in the porno had totally dominated the woman and made the act of love look like a violent act of hate. It was the most terrible, shocking thing I ever saw. I don't know why I wanted Patrick to have sex with me like this in my fantasy.

I was so repulsed by what I wanted.

He was my husband, but I wanted him to be someone else.

A complete stranger.

A rapist.

"No!" my mind screamed as the fantasy mutated into a glowing taboo. I tried to change it back to what it was before my darkest desires rushed in, but I was up against a force far too powerful; and as I tried to make myself think something else, what I was thinking commanded me to continue thinking it. The moment Patrick morphed into

54

a rapist what I was feeling where I was touching myself became overwhelming, turning from just a nice, pleasant feeling into pure pleasure, pleasure squared, pleasure multiplying itself times itself over and over in a repeating equation building towards orgasm. I stopped trying to not think the bad thoughts and submitted totally to their dominance over my mind and body. And it was like I could see my orgasm in my mind before it arrived, surging up from wherever it came from to where it would explode through my body. When it finally came it swallowed me whole. I was inside it inside me. The universe disappeared, and my orgasm became all that was.

Until it wasn't.

And then an angel spoke to me.

"Thou shalt not commit adultery."

When the words hit my ears it felt like I'd been hurtled from my bed and slammed against the wall. But I was still in bed, in bed, where I had done the most awful thing imaginable; where I had done what the angels had seen. My heart felt like it was pumping pure liquid shame through my veins instead of blood.

I was so, so, so ashamed.

The shame was enormous. It was too big for my body. It expanded to fill the room, the house, then the entire world, and continued to spread out from there to fill outer space; my shame was larger than this or any world. My shame was everything and I was all of it; my shame was my orgasm turned upside down, its pleasure removed, revealing its true form, a wolf in sheep's clothing showing itself for what it really was with an ominous howl: the sound of sin under my skin.

I was my sin.

I was what I had done.

As I ruminated in my guilt, a frantic-sounding voice different from all the other angel voices I'd heard before shouted, "Why? Why did you do it? Why! Why! Why!"

"I don't know," I said as franticly as the voice I'd just heard. "I didn't want to do it. I knew it was a sin. I'm so sorry. Please forgive me!"

"Why did you do it?", the frantic voiced angel asked again.

"I don't know. I just did it. I didn't mean to," I said so loudly I thought I might wake my parents and my sister. Then, lowering my voice, I said, "It was an accident."

"Thou shalt not commit adultery," repeated the angel from before.

"But I didn't," I said. "I'm a virgin. I'm saving myself for marriage. I will only ever have sex with my husband. I'm so sorry. I wasn't thinking."

"Yes you were," said an angel. "We saw what you were thinking."

When the angel said that, I saw Patrick and me, naked in my bed, inside my head, again. The angels had watched everything. They had witnessed as he turned from my husband into a stranger then into a rapist.

They saw it all.

"That wasn't Patrick," said the frantic angel voice. "It was the devil!"

"The devil!" I cried in a panic as my shame became terror. The devil had been in my head as I touched my vagina? Had he come to me disguised in the form of a fantasy about Patrick?

Could this be true?

"He wants you for his wife," screamed the frantic angel.

"The devil?" I asked.

"Yes," an angel answered. "He wants you to have his child."

The new world that had replaced my old one when the angels first came took on a new dimension. In this world I spoke to angels, I was a prophet, the devil wanted my soul, and now, there was a new addition: he wanted me to be his wife, to have his baby.

The Antichrist.

But I thought God had chosen me to be His prophet for a special purpose. Now it seemed the situation had been re-served. It was the devil that wanted me for a special reason: to birth his child. But what did this mean? What about the angels? They worked for God. Where did they fit in? Surely they wouldn't let the devil's plan come to fruition. The angels were there to help. Weren't they? Weren't they fighting against the devil for God?

The devil. He was the temptation to sin, I realized. That's how he got in.

Wanting to sin was him in me.

Was he still in my head now that the fantasy was over?

"He wants you for his wife!" the angel repeated in a shout.

"I don't want to be his wife," I said.

"Then never do that again," said an angel.

"I wont. I promise," I said.

"Tell God that," said an angel.

Hadn't God already heard me make my promise right then? I thought I could feel His penetrating gaze looking right through me down from heaven, seeing every thought I thought and every feeling I felt, just like the angels could.

I was completely naked with no way to cover up.

"Pray to Jesus for forgiveness," an angel said. "And ask Him to save you from the devil."

I began to pray inside my head hearing an angel echo my thoughts: "God, I'm sorry. Please forgive me."

"God wants to know what your sorry for," said an angel.

Didn't He already know, I wondered? Didn't He know what I was going to say before I said it? Didn't He even know what I thought before I thought it? Didn't He know everything?

"He wants to hear you say it," said an angel in response to my wondering.

"God, I'm sorry for touching myself," the echoing angel said out loud to God as I thought it in my head.

"For touching yourself where?" an angel asked.

I didn't understand why the angels, and therefore God, wanted me to be so specific. Didn't they know what I meant? Why did I have to say it?

"He wants to hear you say it," said an angel in the same words as before.

The sound of my prayer thoughts coming back to me in the voice of an angel was like a dark cloud hanging over me raining down shame. It was a sound I felt, as I prayed, "God, I'm sorry for touching my vagina," and as I heard this line of thought repeated by the mimicking angel I felt a strange, uncomfortable sensation in my vagina as if it didn't belong there and knew it and was trying to shrink away, disappear.

After I apologized to God for touching my vagina, an angel broke into my prayer and said, "Call it what they did in the video."

The video! Instantly I knew what video the angel was referring to. The porno. It was the most disturbing thing I had ever seen. Every clip from every scene was burned into my memory.

"That's when the devil entered you," said an angel.

Satan was in me? Right then at that moment?

This truth I had just learned moments ago sank in deeper as I remembered the video. What the angel had said about it meant the devil hadn't just entered me tonight in the form of a sexual fantasy about Patrick; he had been in me for a long time. He wasn't coming for me. He was already there. For years I'd carried with me a vague feeling, something like a premonition of bad things to come, and now this feeling had a name: the devil.

"He wants your soul as much as God does," said an angel.

"He wants you for his wife!" said the frantic angel, who was beginning to sound like a parrot that only knew how to say one thing.

"They are fighting for your soul," said an angel.

"Now say it!" commanded another angel in a voice that reminded me of my dad's when he was angry about something.

"I'm sorry, God, for touching my vagina," I prayed in my head.

"No! Call it what they did in the video," the angel demanded.

What they wanted me to say dawned on me in the midst of the confusion I had developed over what the angels had asked me to do. Why did they want me to use that word in prayer to God? Why would angels make me do something like that? Why couldn't I just call it my vagina?

"He wants to hear you say it," an angel said again.

"But why?" I asked. I didn't want to say that word.

In response to my question an angel said what my mom always said when I asked her something about why things were a certain way. The angel said, "God works in mysterious ways. Now say it to God."

I didn't want to say it. But I had to. The angels were ordering me to and their orders came from God. What I wanted was not what God wanted, and what He wanted mattered more than what I wanted, so I followed the instructions of the angels and began to think in prayer with the horrible word the angels demanded I say seeming to glow like a neon light in my mind. But this time, there was no echo; the angel was silent.

Why?

"He wants to hear you say it with your mouth," said an angel.

Again, I wondered why.

"Do not question the Lord your God," lectured an angel.

"Now say it," said another.

"God", I said, my voice sounding odd to my ears, like it wasn't my voice, as it made its way up to God, "please forgive me for touching…my…pussy."

When I said the word pussy it felt like a clump of mud had dropped from my mouth and landed on my chest with a thud covering me in dirt. Just like how my sin had made me feel like I was my sin, saying that word, pussy, made me feel like I was what I'd said.

A dirty, awful thing.

The word pussy sounded alien coming out of my mouth like someone else was saying it, and this feeling was increased by hearing an angel in the background repeat what I'd said up to God.

Pussy out my mouth into my ears where I heard what God heard.

It was the first time that word had ever left my lips.

I had never said it. Not ever.

I had heard other people say it, and when they did, even though it felt silly and immature to want to do this, I wanted to cover my ears the way my mom used to tell me to do when we were watching a movie where one of the actors used a bad word she knew was in it. My mom never let me watch anything more than PG when I was little until she watched it first and judged it OK for my eyes and ears, but she would always chime in at the bad parts directing me to cover my ears or cover my eyes if a nude scene was coming up.

I wanted to cover my eyes and ears right then. I wanted to bury my head in the sand. I wanted to go somewhere where I would be alone, where God and the angels could not see me. It was a desire to blink out of existence, because anywhere I went they would be there.

They were where I was.

Always.

I wanted to be invisible to them right then, to become what they couldn't see.

The shock of the moment began to evaporate, but the word pussy was still present hovering somewhere in the silence, threatening to become a sound again, something I'd said waiting to be said again. I could feel the word in the air around me and could sense its desire to be spoken aloud again as if it had a will of its own, but I didn't want to say it, not ever again, and I wished and wished that the angels would not ask me to say it again.

Then an angel spoke in a voice I hadn't heard before, different from the angel voices I had become accustomed to. It was a mean-spirited, mocking voice, and it said, "Lisa, are you a little slut?"

This was almost word for word what one of the guys in the porno had asked the woman he was doing sick things to with his penis. I was smacked in the head by this comment. Big time. My mind was blown.

It was like this one time with my mom, the way I felt right then. My mom had only smacked me once in my life. I was thirteen and I said something fresh to her. As I was coming into my teenage years, my mother and I were drifting apart. We'd been so close when I was growing up. I was a momma's girl, always clinging to her, like at the park, when the other children were running around, chasing one another, and playing on the monkey bars, I would be in my mother's lap watching them all. My mom seemed to love being who I wanted her to be; she was everything to me, and I felt like the most important thing in the world to her, but then Samantha came and everything changed after she was born. My mom started talking about how I had to be a big girl now, and she would refuse me when I would try to climb up into her lap. I wasn't her special little girl anymore. The way she acted towards me changed overnight, it seemed.

I thought this meant she didn't love me anymore.

Looking back, I see that my mom purposely tried to distance herself from me for my own good. I was growing up. I couldn't always go to my mom for every little thing. I had to learn to stand on my own two feet. Even so, as our connection became less and less, it hurt a lot. I began to resent her and my baby sis, and even almost hate them both, keeping this feeling in that secret place within that I told you about, where the other Lisa lived and harbored all my secrets. When my mom slapped me when I was thirteen, it stung a little but not a lot; what really hit me was the shock, the total surprise. My mom's hand, once a tender thing that had held me and patted me gently to sleep when I was a baby had become a weapon, a thing of violence. When the angel asked me if I was a slut that's what it felt like: being slapped by a hand that had cradled me since birth.

Everything I had thought prior to this moment about the angels was thrown out of whack. It didn't make any sense. Why would the angels call me a prophet one day and then call me a slut another day? In my mind I thought the angels said what God thought. Did God think I was a slut? Had He changed his mind about me being a prophet when He spied me masturbating?

Masturbating.

My terrible sin.

No prophet masturbated; that was something a slut did. But being a prophet didn't seem like something you could be one day and not the next. It was something you were, a part of you that couldn't be erased, or so I thought. But a slut was also something you either were or were not, and you couldn't be a slut and a prophet at the same time, could you? Didn't one cancel the other out? I didn't really know what a prophet did, but I knew what a slut did. She slept with lots of boys. I didn't do that. I thought about it sometimes, but I would never act on that thought. But I had, I realized, I'd touched my vagina and given myself an orgasm. That was something a slut did, but I didn't want to do it, it was a mistake; no, I wasn't a real slut.

But why would an angel call me a slut if it weren't true?

"Some of us work for God," said an angel, "and some of us work for the devil."

So God's angels didn't call me a slut then?

"It's a game for your soul," said another angel.

This changed everything. I wasn't only hearing angels from heaven but also ones from hell. This added another twist to this new reality that had come one Sunday night when an angel had spoken to me. I had been so excited about hearing angels, but that's when I thought they were all God's angels. I didn't want to hear the devil's angels. I only wanted what was from heaven, the good, to be there with me.

This revelation that the devil's minions were trying to influence my life in service of him weighted me down, sinking me lower than I already was feeling, to a place in me where the guilt and shame of being caught masturbating by the angels, and God, gathered into a thick, thought-trapping cloud that emitted flashes of terror, which came and went like strikes of lighting each time I thought about the devil and his evil angels.

"He wants you for his wife," said the angel with the frantic voice that I was starting to loathe.

Then another angel asked, "Why did you say that word to God?"

I knew what word he meant: pussy.

"They told me to," I said

"That was the devil's angel. Why did you listen to it?" said an angel.

"I didn't know. I'm sorry," I said in a desperate voice.

As the words left my lips I felt something ripple through me. It was a familiar feeling yet I couldn't remember when I'd felt it before. It came in waves. I felt it on my skin at first; then the feeling reverberated into my body, exiting just as it returned to the surface of my skin on its way back in. It was a horrible feeling. When it hit my skin the hair on my arms stood up, my skin got all itchy like I was having an allergic reaction, and once inside the feeling manifested into dread that I experienced in a dizzying state of vertigo while my chest felt like it was being crushed under the weight of a demolished building. What felt like currents of electricity passed through my head from temple to temple, scrambling my thoughts into a disordered jumble.

The dread, the strange, otherworldly sensation, seemed to be flowing into my body from an invisible presence situated all around me in the darkness of my room. I pushed my head under my covers with the rest of my body and held the blanket closed tight with my hands so there was no opening, wrapping myself in a cocoon. I remember seeing a TV show once, I forget which one, where a kid was afraid of monsters under his bed that he believed were going to come out and get him at night, and to comfort him his dad told him that everyone knew monsters can't get you if you stay hidden under your covers. I guess a blanket was to monsters what a crucifix and a silver bullet are to vampires and werewolves. I wasn't really trying to hide from anything by wrapping myself all up in my blankets, but I was trying to block the dreadful vibe the mysterious something in my room was emitting from it into me, to keep it from entering my body. It was a failed attempt. I still felt whatever it was pulsating its eerie vibration through the blankets where it passed through the pores on my skin and filled my body with a sensation I visualized as a dark, oozing substance like a liquid shadow.

Was what I saw in my mind what was in my body, or was I just imagining it? Maybe it was something worse than what I thought it was. Worse than anything I could possibly imagine, a fear so frightening you could fear it without knowing what it was you were afraid of.

This presence needed a name.

"He wants you for his wife," said the frantic angel the instant I realized its name; the name of this presence in my room.

The devil.

He had finally come for me. He was there in my room. If I ran from my room he would follow in my footsteps as close behind as my shadow at my side, or maybe he would be steps ahead, already knowing where I was going, like my shadow cast in a certain light stretched out in front of me, pointing towards my destination, where the devil would be waiting for me to arrive.

All this I was thinking spiraled down into a terrible re-alization: if the devil was where I was and anywhere I could go, then he had already taken me away. The angels had told me that wasn't Patrick in my head, it was the devil; he had come in and stolen me away to a dark place filled with false, colorful lights that swirled into the illusion of Patrick and me, husband and wife, making love, sweet and beautiful at first, until the devil took off his Patrick mask, so he was no longer disguised as my fantasy husband but was now a stranger. As this was revealed to me everything darkened so I could only see a whirl of shadows when I looked up at the devil's face as he raped me, in my mind, as my fingers violated my vagina, without me telling them to, as if my hands were under the devil's spell while my body was pos-sessed with his presence.

Realizing the devil had raped me in my head sent me into a panic. It was really him; he was real. He was here in my room and he wanted my soul and he wanted to marry me and have me give birth to his child, the Antichrist. It was all too much to think about at once. My heart began pounding so loudly I thought I could hear it, and when I thought about how the devil could also hear it, since he was in the room with me, my heart began to beat even louder, banging against my ribcage it felt like, as if trying to es-cape from my body, a thump, thump, thumping, beating its way up my throat into my mouth where it would jump out and run away from what being inside me made it feel like.

I didn't know what to do.

"I bet you want to touch your pussy again," said an angel that I knew was from hell.

"Never do that again," said an angel I imagined was from heaven telling me what God wanted me to hear.

"I wont. I swear," I said.

"Yes you will, you're a little slut," said an angel I just knew was from down below.

Slut.

When I heard the word it sounded like how a paper cut felt.

Being called it made me feel ugly inside.

I wanted this to end.

"Pray," said an angel of God. "Pray to make the devil go away."

I did exactly that.

As quickly as possible, I eagerly prayed my way to the final word: amen. I hoped that saying this word would magically make the angels go away like it had the other two times they'd come.

But after I said amen an angel said, "The devil is leaving. God is making it so."

Hearing this brought relief that was cut short for a brief moment when an angel from hell said, "We'll be back. He is always watching you."

"He wants you for his wife," said the mockingbird angel again.

Then the devils angels were gone. I knew this not just through their sudden silence, but I felt it like a sixth sense; they were gone, along with the devil, back down in hell.

"That's where they belong," said an angel I felt was on my side. "You don't want to go there do you?"

"No! I want to go to heaven! I want God to win!" I exclaimed referring to the battle between God and the devil for my soul.

"Then never do that again," the angel responded.

"I never will. Not ever. I promise you. I promise God," I swore to the angels and God.

The Fork in the Road

The night felt like it would never end.

I couldn't sleep.

I lay still in bed trying to erase what I'd done from my memory. All was quiet. I was glad. I didn't want to talk about what I had done with the angels anymore. I had prayed to God for forgiveness, and I was truly sorry, and God forgave all who humbly came to Him in confession of their sins. I knew God had forgiven me, but I still felt terrible. I wished I could go back in time and stop myself from doing what I'd done. Most of all I just wanted to stop thinking about it. And I wanted to know what God really thought about me now.

Was I still a prophet?

I asked the angels this and one said yes back. This boosted my depleted sense of self-worth a little bit, and I was happy to change the subject away from my sinful act, so I asked, "What does it mean that I'm a prophet? What am I supposed to do?"

"You are going to deliver a message from God to the world after what is going to happen is over," said an angel.

"What's going to happen?" I asked.

"You're a prophet," said an angel.

What kind of answer was this? Did the angel mean prophets could see the future? They could, couldn't they? The Bible was full of stories of people blessed by God with prophetic wisdom. God would show them what was going to happen so they could warn everyone else. It was just like how Noah warned people about the flood.

"You're a prophet," repeated the angel, and I took this as an answer to my questions, a confirmation telling me I was right, I could see the future.

Was this ability, the power to see the future, something I had suddenly acquired, or had I always been clairvoyant and not realized it? I looked back at my life for evidence that I had perceived events in advance of them happening. At first nothing major stood out, but then I began to think about how everyone I knew always seemed to say exactly what I thought they were going to say. People's responses usually matched my expectations. I could always guess what would happen next in a movie. I knew when my mom was in a bad mood even before she said anything angry towards me. I would feel it on the bus ride home from school: Mom is going to be in a bad mood today, I would think, and I would see her upset in my mind before I saw her in person, reacting just as I had anticipated.

All the time when I listened to the radio I would think of a song right before they played it. One time I was in the car with my mom when a song I had just been thinking about came on, and I said, "Wow! I was just thinking about this song," and my mom said, "Isn't it crazy when coincidences like that happen?" After she said this I labeled this phenomenon I had experienced repeatedly as a coincidence, like my mom had said.

But maybe she was wrong.

Maybe when I thought of a song before it came on the radio I was catching a small glimpse into the future.

Also, I always knew what kind of day it was going to be when I woke up.

When I'd woken up in the morning of this day I'm writing about now, I had a bad feeling. This feeling persisted throughout the day. I thought about Patrick a lot during the day for some reason, and when I did, I wanted to touch myself; and when I felt this desire, I saw an image in my mind of me doing this. As thoughts like these increased, so did the ominous feeling I had woken up with that morning. I didn't know this feeling was connected to my thoughts of Patrick and thoughts of me touching myself.

I didn't realize that I was sensing the future.

Seeing in my head what I would later do in my bed that night.

What the devil would make me do.

How far into the future could I see? I wondered.

What were the limitations of this God-given gift?

Right then, when I thought about the future, trying to look as far into it as I could, I saw two dueling visions. In one I did what the angel of God had just told me I was going to do: a vision of me delivering a message from God to the world: and in another my belly was swollen with the devil's offspring; the devil, who was my husband, and the owner of my soul, in this vision of terror.

Which vision was the real one?

God must know. God knew everything.

I tried to get this information from God's head by asking the angels which vision of the future I saw was the real one, but silence was the only answer my question received.

"Hello?" I asked.

No reply.

The angels were gone.

For now.

The rest of the night I tossed and turned in my bed trying to fall asleep. My emotions shot all over the place. Each moment had its own color, its own emotion. I would be high one second and low the next, feeling as restless in bed as I did in my head, as this rapid cycle of emotions pulled me every which way. I felt one emotion come as its opposite left, and what I was feeling seemed to radiate from my thoughts. My mind was split down the middle. I was thinking in two directions, thinking thoughts of hope that took me up to where I wanted to be and thoughts of fear that dragged me down to a place I wanted to escape: the two futures I saw wrestling in my mind.

When I saw the future where I was a prophet delivering God's message to the world I swelled with hope, and when I saw the future where I was the devil's wife and the mother of his child, it sucked all the good feelings out from me and filled me with despair. I would be floating in elation one moment and falling in terror in the next. Up and down, down and up, on and on it went like this, this same drama playing itself out in my mind over and over, what I wanted fighting what I didn't. It was a battle between the two futures I saw, what I hoped would happen opposing what I was scared would happen. All I could do was watch as these two forces fought in my head, racing towards the finish line that ended where the future began. I was in the present, the past was behind me, and the future was up ahead where it was becoming what would eventually be. My twin visions, one good, the other evil, competed against each other in a battle to see which one would become reality.

It was the war for my soul. The outcome of the future.

What a night it had been; a terrible awful night.

What else can I say?

The devil had raped me in my head that night. He had done to me what I had done to me. He was the temptation and the sin. And he had tricked me into saying pussy to God. What else? He wanted my soul. He wanted me to be his wife. He wanted to impregnate me with the Antichrist. Why me? Out of all the girls in the world, why choose me to be his wife? Why was the devil so interested in me? Why was God? What was it about me? I had no idea. But I was certain I would never touch my vagina inappropriately again.

I wanted God to win.

I fell asleep with a war in my head that ended where a peaceful dream began.

A dream where everything was exactly what I wanted it to be.

Beauty and the Beast

Before I tell you what took place the morning after that awful night, I want to tell you about something that happened when I was six. That was when I saw that disgusting video. The porno. I learned what sex was from it. Before I saw it the only image of sex that I had came from a girl named Mary who went to the same baby-sitter as me. She told me sex was when the husband takes off his wife's clothes and the wife takes off her husband's clothes before they lie down in bed together and kiss, and that's how babies were made, that's what she told me, word for word. She didn't say boy or girl, or woman and man, she said husband and wife, and they somehow produced a baby by kissing without clothes on while in bed. I didn't understand how this was possible. I instinctively knew something was missing from the picture Mary had painted in my mind, but I didn't know what that something was. I had questions but I didn't know what those questions were. It was like that. But even though it didn't make sense to me, I believed Mary. She was a year older than me and she always seemed to know all about the stuff adults tried to keep secret from us. She knew what all the naughty words really meant, or at least she claimed to. Once, after listening in a state of absolute shock as she gave the definition of a number of obscenities, I told on her. Yes, I was a tattletale. I thought she needed her mouth washed out with soap, and that's what I hoped her mom would do when she found out, but the next day Mary bragged to me that her mom didn't care, and she could use any word she wanted to around her. I tried to imagine what her house must be like and couldn't. Mary scared me, I guess, looking back, because every little thing she said to me stole a piece of my innocence. It seemed like her favorite pastime, something she thought was so much fun: telling me what I wasn't supposed to know.

Mary was the first person to touch the inside of my vagina. She stuck her finger in me and wiggled it around. I had never done that before to myself. We were playing doctor and I was the patient. Mary said she was checking me for cancer after getting me to pull my pants down. Mary's finger in me didn't feel bad, it just felt strange, like nothing I'd ever felt before, and a feeling spread from where she was touching me to all over my body, making me feel weird inside. Yet I didn't want her to stop for some reason; the feeling she was causing in me had a mysterious attraction to it, a certain magnetism that pulled me deeper into its sensation. I wanted to explore this sensation some more, so I started doing what Mary had done to me to myself, at home, alone in my room. Somehow I knew it was wrong, but once I started doing things to myself down there I couldn't stop. It became an addiction of sorts, or maybe you could call it a hobby, something I did when I was bored and alone. I didn't get orgasms from what I did; that wouldn't come until much later, until after puberty hit. That didn't matter, I didn't know what an orgasm was, I didn't even know that what I was doing to myself was sexual, because I didn't know what sex was. I just liked how it felt to feel around inside my vagina, touching all the sensitive areas that liked to be touched.

It was also because of Mary that I first learned what a divorce was. Her parents became divorced after Mary's mother discovered that her husband had been molesting their daughter. Mary's dad had to go to prison because of this. I didn't find out about all this until I was much older. At the time, when I asked my mom why Mary's dad had to go away, she told me it was because he did something evil to Mary. When I asked my mom what that evil thing Mary's dad did to her was, my mom told me I wasn't old enough to know yet. If my mom said that, then I didn't want to know, but at the same time I did; I was a curious kid. I knew she was protecting me from something awful, doing the opposite of what Mary did to me when she told me about bad stuff; my mom was preserving my innocence. I didn't know what innocence was, the word was not in my limited six-year-old vocabulary, but I clung to mine, as if it were what I was, and would no longer be once it left me.

But there was also something within me that was drawn to anything that threatened my innocence; I vaguely sensed it, even at that age, as something dark in me that I didn't think of as a part of me but as something hostile and intrusive that came from outside my self.

It was around this time that I first started having night-mares about the devil.

So, anyways, since my mom wouldn't tell me what Mary's dad did to her. I figured Mary would tell me at the baby-sitters, but she didn't, to my relief-tinged disappointment. I wanted to know what I didn't want to know; my innocence shrank back from the taboo my mom was trying to keep out of my head, while my curiosity reached out for this forbidden fruit. Like I told you before, I was real shy. I would have never asked Mary what her dad did to her even though a part of me wanted to. All I could do was wait for Mary to tell me herself, but she never talked about it. In fact, she stopped talking all together, for the most part, and instead of playing outside with me, she would sit in the baby-sitter's house quietly watching cartoons. I didn't like playing by myself. Being alone frightened me for some reason, so I started staying inside watching cartoons with Mary, who seemed so different than she'd been before. The confident Mary who had boldly proclaimed to me everything I wasn't supposed to know was gone. Now she seemed frail. If you blew on her it would knock her over. That's how she seemed. And she always had a guilty look on her face like she'd done something really awful that she regretted having done. Sometimes when we were watching cartoons she wouldn't even be looking at the TV screen, but would instead stare down at the floor where her legs were twisted together into a knot.

She was looking at something that wasn't there.

Seeing something I could not see.

And I didn't want to see it. I didn't want to know what she knew, and I sensed that she didn't either. Before she had been so proud of her mental catalog of sinful facts that she relished passing on to me, but now it was like she had shut down from having learned one awful truth too many. She looked trapped inside herself, and whatever it was that made her stay inside instead of playing outside in the sunshine with me, I didn't want to know, because I feared knowing would make me like her. I was no longer scared of her. I felt pity for her and I didn't know what to do with this pity. It was something I did not enjoy feeling, so I tried to make it go away by being extra nice to Mary. But every nice act towards her and every kind word I spoke to her, seemed to have no effect; it was like my words turned into nothing in her ears, and there was something about her that made her seem untouchable, like you could pat her on the back and she wouldn't feel a thing.

That's how she seemed.

The baby-sitter had a pool in the backyard, and when summer came Mary and I were permitted to swim in it as long as Jane, the baby-sitter, was there to supervise us. It was a beautiful summer day and I was excited to swim, but Mary just wanted to stay inside and watch cartoons. Jane began trying to persuade her to go for a swim, telling her how much fun it would be and how good the water was going to feel. Still Mary didn't budge. She said she wanted to watch Beauty and the Beast. It was her favorite movie, I knew, because I had watched it a bunch of times with her, and back before when she was still the old Mary she used to sing along with all the ballads she had memorized from the movie. She would say, "Come on, Lisa, sing with me," with a big smile on her face, and I would, I would sing along with her, and this would seem to make her happy.

I didn't want to go in the pool alone. I wanted to have a playmate. I wanted Mary to be Mary again, and I hoped maybe once she got in the pool, she would magically turn back to her old self, and we could play Marco Polo or see who could stay underwater and hold their breath the longest. So in an attempt to coax her outside, I said, "Mary, if you come swimming, I'll watch Beauty and the Beast with you, and we can sing along with all the songs." She got a thoughtful look on her face. It had been a long time since I'd seen anything but a flat expression on her face. Then she began to look at me. She was sitting on the floor in front of the TV and I was there with Jane standing over Mary looking down at her with a smile. "Come on," I said. "It will be fun."

Then Mary's eyes got wide as if she was realizing something. She looked up at me and her eyes narrowed into two slits that made her look like she was mad at me, and she said, "I don't want to watch Beauty and the Beast anymore. I brought a different movie."

"We can watch whatever you want. Just come swimming," I said.

"I'll go swimming with you if you watch the video with me," she said.

"OK, but swimming first," I said.

"OK," she said.

"Yippee!" I shouted, pulling her by the hand to get her to stand up. "Go put on your bathing suit."

Mary changed in the bathroom. My swimsuit was already on. I was ready to go with inflated bright orange floaties ballooned around my tiny biceps because I wasn't that strong of a swimmer yet. Mary didn't need any floaties and she seemed to make a big show of this on purpose by diving down and touching the bottom of the deep end over and over, each time coming up, saying, "Look, I touched the bottom." Her tone of voice had a superior air to it. She was beginning to remind me of the old Mary. She made touching the bottom sound like the greatest feat one could possibly accomplish, and it made me slightly jealous that I couldn't do it. My floaties kept me buoyed at the surface and every time I tried to go down deep the air in my floaties would send me shooting back up.

"You can't do it with your floaties on," said Mary. "Take them off."

"I'm not supposed to," I responded.

"You can swim, can't you?" Mary asked.

"Yes. I can swim. But my mom doesn't let me go in a big pool without my floaties," I answered.

"Well, your mom's not here," she said. When Mary said this I caught a glimpse into an unfamiliar reality where the rules of your mother did not apply when she was not there with you.

In my world it was like my mom was there even when she wasn't.

The rules of my parents walled the world up into a maze that separated what I could do from what I couldn't, and this maze didn't just disappear when my parents weren't around. It remained, its walls invisible, but I could feel them all around me as I tried to stay within the lines; and if ever I took a wrong step, did something I was not supposed to, I would smack into one of these invisible walls, feeling not a physical pain from it but an emotional one: the feeling of disappointment. It didn't feel like my own feeling. It felt like I was feeling what my parents would feel towards me if they had been there to witness what I'd done, and my thoughts would then become critical towards myself and would begin to resemble one of my parents' lectures.

So what could I say to Mary, as she continued her attempt to get me to remove my floaties so I could touch the bottom with her? She already knew that I wasn't supposed to take them off because my mom said so, and this didn't seem to matter to her. "I can do whatever I want," she said, as if bragging, sounding more and more like her old self. "I bet your mom doesn't let you cross the street unless she's holding your hand," she said.

"No," I said, "that's not true. I just have to look both ways before I cross."

Waving her arms and feet underwater to stay on level with where my floaties kept me on the surface, Mary said proudly, "I don't have to look both ways. I just cross."

"What about cars?" I asked.

"I don't care," she said, "I'm not scared of getting hit by one."

After Mary said this it somehow made her seem more powerful, fearless.

Before I had a chance to respond to what she'd just said, Mary started trying to get me take off my floaties again, saying, "I promise, I won't let you drown. I'll take you down with me. I'll hold on to you. And then we can go back up together."

I didn't know how to say no to her. I looked to Jane who was laid out on a reclined patio chair letting herself tan in the sun. She wasn't paying attention to us. I had hoped that she would've been when I looked up at her, because if she'd been listening she would've told Mary I wasn't allowed to take my floaties off because that's what my mom had told her. But Jane was oblivious to us.

What to do? What to do? I wondered and wondered.

And then a sudden burst of inspiration rushed into my mind with just the right idea. I said to Mary, "OK. I'll go to the bottom with you, but I've got to ask Jane first if it's OK to take off my floaties."

Mary reluctantly agreed to this because she knew what I knew, that Jane would say no. And that's exactly what she said when I asked her if it was OK to remove my floaties: no.

Mary began to argue with her, "Aww, come on," she pleaded. "I'll hold on to her the whole time and won't let go."

"No, sorry, kid," said Jane. "Lisa's mom said she could only go in the pool with her floaties on. It's up to her. Not me. And I have to do what she says, because she's my boss"; and after she said this she went back into her little bubble, dark sunglasses over her eyes, her body all oily with tanning lotion, her head back, looking up towards the sky, and not at us.

"Fine. Whatever," Mary said in a let-down voice, but then her tone suddenly got enthusiastic as she said in accelerated speech. "Since you can't swim down with me to the bottom you have to come watch the video instead."

I didn't want to get out of the pool yet, but there was something domineering in Mary's personality at that moment. It had a hypnotizing effect on me somehow, that made me feel submissive, like I had to do whatever she wanted to.

"OK. I'll go inside and watch cartoons with you," I said.

" "This video isn't a cartoon. It's something else," she said.

"Is it as good as Beauty and the Beast?" I asked.

"It's just different. It's like nothing you've seen before. I promise," she said.

I was beginning to get curious, "OK," I said. "Let's go watch it."

Mary quickly splashed her way to the steps and climbed out of the pool as I followed slowly.

"We're going in," Mary announced to Jane just as I was making my way out of the pool onto the warm, pebbled patio.

Jane, without making any motion to look at either of us, said, "You kids make sure you towel off before you go inside. And make sure you dry your feet, too. I don't want to drive you to the hospital because one of you slipped on one of the tiles and cracked your head open."

"OK, we will," said Mary, speaking for me, as well as for herself, and I don't know why, but right then, having her speak for me felt natural, like the right thing. I had a queer feeling as I moved forward following behind Mary after we'd toweled off and were making our way into the house. What I was feeling wasn't like a bad feeling or a sense that something horrible was going to happen; it was much more intangible than that, like I was letdown in someone else's dream. That's how I felt for some reason as I went where Mary went, into Jane's room where the VCR and TV were, and where Mary had her Disney backpack that had a big picture of Beauty dancing with the Beast on the front of it. She unzipped it open and pulled out a black videocassette that had no label on it of any kind, which made it seem even more mysterious.

Mary cradled it in her palms like she was holding a Cabbage Patch doll as she looked down at it. I looked down at it, too, asking her, "What is it?"

"You'll see," she said as she hit eject on the VCR and pulled out the tape of Beauty and the Beast that had been in there from before. She put it back in its colorful case, which resembled her backpack, and placed it on the dresser.

And as she put the mysterious tape into the VCR, Mary said, "I used to watch this with my dad. It was his favorite," and then she pressed play and sat down on the floor Indian style and patted the carpet next to her. "Come down here," she said, and I did, sitting right next to her so our knees touched while both our backs were leaning up against the end of Jane's bed.

The TV filled with zigzagging streaks of white static that were moving up and down across a pitch black screen.

"There's something wrong with the video," I said.

"No," said Mary, "it just starts out like this then gets better. You'll see."

The video distortion slowly faded away. What I saw next would eventually become my most vivid childhood memory. The first clear image that came into view was of three naked, headless men standing in a circle around a naked blond woman with really big boobs. She was down on her knees. The video seemed to be starting in the middle of something. I didn't know what that something was or what had happened before the people in the video had taken off their clothes. What stood out the most to me were the men's penises. Their heads were cut off from the camera so you could only tell them apart by the individual characteristics of their large, long penises that were pointing straight at the woman. The only penis I had ever seen before was my dad's. I'd walked into my parents' room one day and my dad was standing there naked, fresh out of the shower. His penis didn't look like the ones the guys had in the video. His was much smaller and shriveled up, hanging down towards the ground, and not pointing up in the air. Later my dad explained to me what I saw. He said his penis was where his pee came out from, and he told me I didn't have one, because I was a girl. That was my first definition of a penis. Something pee came out of that only boys had. My dad's penis had looked soft and harmless. I didn't know my dad's penis could become hard and grow like the ones in the video. I didn't know what an erection was. I thought my dad's penis stayed the way it was always and I thought the only thing he used it for was to pee.

But the headless men in the video were not using their penises to pee. They were doing other things with it. The woman kneeling down on the floor was eagerly sucking on the men's hard penises. She had a smile on her face as she did this, switching from penis to penis, making an "mmm" sound as she sucked, as if the men's penises tasted good in her mouth. She looked like she really enjoyed what she was doing. It seemed like there was something she wanted that was somewhere inside the men's penises that she was trying to work out with her mouth.

Was she drinking pee out of their penises? I wondered.

That would be gross, I thought. Why would she want to get pee in her mouth?

Then the headless man currently being sucked on by the big-breasted blond, said to her, "Yeah, bitch, suck that cock."

Cock. It was the first time I had ever heard that word. I realized he was using it to refer to his penis the woman was sucking on, and that's what it became in my mind, a cock, no longer a penis; my dad had a penis, but these men had cocks.

And I didn't understand why the man had called the woman a bitch. I didn't know what that word meant, but I knew it was a bad word, and that calling someone it was an insult; but the woman didn't seem to mind being addressed this way, which was perplexing to me. She just continued sucking with a look of pure joy on her face.

She was holding one cock with one of her hands as she sucked on it while she stroked the cock of another man with her other hand. The third guy stood over her holding his own cock, which he was slapping against the face of the woman over and over as if he were trying to hurt her with it.

The men's cocks began to seem like weapons to me. They were the most potent looking objects I had ever seen. I stared at them in shock and amazement as they glowed off the TV screen. They looked dangerous; they frightened me. I wanted to cover my eyes and plug my ears but something wouldn't let me. It was as if the video had a power over me. Just like how my floaties had pushed me up to the waters surface every time I'd tried to dive down in the pool, the video somehow pulled my eyes back to the TV screen every time I tried to look away.

The more I looked at the cocks, the more they seemed to take on a life of their own, separate from the headless men whose bodies they were attached to. The cocks began to resemble some kind of deadly beasts attacking the woman. This confused me because the woman seemed to enjoy it so. It was as if she were down in a pit of vipers completely unafraid, having the time of her life, and when the vipers bit her their poison felt like ecstasy in her veins.

I was so confused.

And what happened in the video next tripled my confusion.

One of the men grabbed the woman by the throat with one hand as if he were trying to choke her, then turned her head to face his direction with his other hand, right before he slapped her hard across the cheek.

"You like sucking dick, don't you," he said.

Dick. Another word I had never heard before. Yet another term for penis.

There was a red mark on the woman's cheek where the man had slapped her. After being slapped she began giggling as if she'd been tickled by the hit. This contradicted everything I thought I knew about physical violence. In my mind being slapped by someone had always been associated with pain. You hit someone when you wanted to hurt them, and being hit by someone hurt. It was a simple equation, but what I saw in the video made this no longer seem like the right answer. Why had the man slapped the woman? Was he mad at her? What had she done to him? And the thing I didn't understand the most was how the woman seemed to enjoy this abuse. A strange new reality began to dawn in me, a window into an alternate universe, where hitting someone brought them pleasure instead of pain and calling someone a bad name like bitch made her happy instead of hurting her feelings.

This threw everything I thought about the universe into disorder. A new explanation was needed to make things make sense again, but I couldn't come up with one, and my confusion only increased the more I tried to solve the bizarre riddle the video had inserted into my mind.

"Are you a little slut?" one of the men asked the woman.

"Yes," answered the woman.

"Tell me what you are," demanded the man who had spoken before.

"I'm a slut," the woman told the man.

Slut. Another word I had never heard before. The video was one long vocabulary lesson of words that would haunt me for the rest of my life. This new word slut came with a definition. The woman had said that's what she was. What was a slut? She was. What did a slut do? A slut did the things she was doing in the video.

Slut.

It was such an awful sounding word, a dirty word that tracked mud into my ears on its way into my head where it covered my mind in filth. It sounded like the name of some evil creature from a fairy tale: Slut.

Next the men began to do new things to the woman with their cocks. The woman was no longer kneeling on the floor but on the bed twisted up in an awkward, uncomfortable looking position, her body tangled up with the bodies of the three men. When the woman first climbed into the bed before the men followed her into it, I wondered if the naked woman was about to be kissed by one of the naked men, thinking of what Mary had told me months ago, before her parents were divorced, when she'd explained what sex was to me. The woman in the video couldn't possibly be married to all these men, I thought, so why would she be trying to make a baby with them? But when the men got into bed with her they did not kiss her; they did other things to her.

One man got on top of her and pushed his hard cock into her vagina, and when he did, the woman said, "Oh, your cock feels so good in my pussy."

Yet another new word: pussy. Just how the word cock had become a word for a scary looking penis that was so unlike the one I'd seen dangling between my dad's legs, the word pussy, what the woman had called her vagina, sounded like a name for a vagina that was more than a vagina. I had a vagina. It was where my pee came out of. The woman in the video had a pussy. In my mind a vagina became a pussy when a man put his cock inside it.

That's how I thought about it.

When the man put his cock inside the woman's pussy, it made me think about the time Mary had put her finger inside me, and made me think about how I had then started to sometimes put my finger inside my vagina the way Mary had put hers in mine. I sensed that these memories were somehow connected to what the man was doing to the woman with his cock, but I wasn't exactly sure how. But as time passed, one impression out of the many this video left on me was that I began to think of my fingers as little cocks when I put them inside my vagina that became a pussy when I did this. After I began to see touching myself in light of what I'd seen in the video, it turned from curious exploration into a shameful act that felt good to do to myself at the same time it filled me with guilt-laced disgust.

While the one man was on top of the woman thrusting his cock into her pussy, another man was sitting underneath her moving his cock in and out of her butt hole. Another ordinary thing was transformed in my mind by the video: the butt hole, the thing your poop came out of, could also have things go into it, like a cock. It was weird to me, but not any weirder than a man putting his cock in a woman's pussy or her mouth; it was all weird to me, and before this video, I had never seen a cock, I had only seen a soft, limp penis, so I had no concept of what a hard cock was or did. What did the video tell me about a cock? It told me a cock did whatever it wanted to do to a naked woman's body.

The third guy was crouched over the woman's face forcing his cock in and out of her mouth as he pushed and pulled her head back and forth so her lips slid up and down his cock, pulling her by the hair as he did this.

The last time I'd remembered having my hair pulled was in preschool. A boy I didn't like did it to me when I wouldn't share the dessert my mom had packed in my lunch for me that day, a cupcake. He pulled my hair and took my cupcake, then ran to the other side of the room where he ravenously gobbled it up in three giant bites. When he pulled my hair it hurt a lot and I cried, but the woman in the video didn't seem to mind having her hair pulled.

It made no sense at all.

The man forcing his cock in and out of the woman's mouth as he pulled her hair brought her face all the way up against him so her forehead touched his belly, and so his cock was all the way in her mouth as deep down as it could go with his scrotum sitting on her chin. The man then pinched the woman's nostrils shut with his thumb and index finger so she couldn't breathe. I started to wonder if he was trying to kill her. The woman had a look of fear in her eyes, and she began to make frantic noises that were muffled by the cock that was pushed deep into her mouth all the way to the back of her throat. She seemed to be trying to shout something. I imagined she was trying to tell the guy to pull his cock out her mouth so she could breathe again, but the guy seemed to have no empathy towards her. He was chuckling as he closed her nostrils shut, like some kind of scary monster, a sociopath who then said to the woman, "Yeah, slut, take it all in, let's see how long you can hold your breath."

The woman began gagging on the man's cock, and she pushed against his abdomen with both her hands, but the man overpowered her, saying, "Had enough?" She continued to try and push him away, while he pushed back with his hips, thrusting them forward, making his cock go down even deeper in her throat, then telling her in an authoritative voice, "I'll tell you when you've had enough, you little slut."

She was at his mercy.

I was frightened for her. Would the guy let her die?

There were two black streaks running down her cheeks from her eyes. She was crying black tears that had been dyed by the dark mascara painted around her eyelids, now all smeared, mixing with her tears as they gathered in her eyes. I began to feel pity for her. I wanted to help her somehow, but she was inside the TV, where I could not reach her. I wanted to shout out at the guy to stop, but my voice was locked up inside me, unable to escape, as if the man's cock were in my mouth, blocking me from saying anything.

When the man finally removed his cock from the woman's mouth she inhaled loudly as I did, too. I'd been holding my breath the whole time. I inhaled deeply as I watched in horror while the man slid his cock out from the woman's mouth, his cock all slimy, covered in the woman's saliva. As the cock exited her mouth, before she began panting in a desperate grab for oxygen, the woman let out a large retching noise that sounded like someone throwing up, and a sizeable spittle of drool oozed out over her lips and dripped down her chin while she gasped and gasped, panting like she'd just sprinted ten miles. Then she grinned up at the man who had just been torturing her with his cock. She looked like she was looking at him in gratitude at what he'd just done to her. He'd almost killed her, I thought. How could she be thankful?

Another question with no answer.

Next the men switched positions. The man who had been choking the woman with his cock took the place of the guy who'd had his cock in her pussy, and that guy took the place of the guy who had his cock in her butt, and the guy who had his cock in her butt positioned himself in a crouch over her face, and without being grabbed, or pulled by the hair, the woman took the man's cock that had been in her butt hole moments ago into her hand voluntarily, as she leaned her neck forward, so she could wrap her lips around the tip of the man's cock. This totally grossed me out. That thing had just come out of her butt, and now she was taking it into her mouth. I thought about how my mom always told me that if I didn't wash my hands after I pooped and then ate afterwards it would make me sick. Did the woman want to make herself sick? Her desires seemed so alien to me, they left me completely baffled; it was like she was from another planet where everything that was wrong or bad on earth was somehow good there. She acted opposite to how I would have. I wanted to know what motivated her. What did those men make her feel like? I wanted to know.

And this desire was soaked in terror.

A part of me that I didn't want in me wanted to feel what the woman felt, to feel her pleasure. I didn't want to want what I wanted. What the men were doing to her looked awful, but the way she reacted made it seem like she was receiving pleasure from this mistreatment. What was hidden from me that I didn't see; where did her pleasure come from? I was confused, and my confusion was my repulsion and curiosity combined. I wanted to know what the men made the woman feel with their three cocks, while the sight of their three monstrous cocks made me want to hide from them, run away to another room; but I couldn't move, I couldn't look away.

Most of all I wanted my confusion to resolve itself somehow. I needed some magic answer to make sense of all this. I felt split in two, like I would never be complete again until I figured out the true meaning of what I was seeing: the secret behind what the woman felt, the beautiful, big-breasted blond who smiled through what looked like torture, her smile that would haunt me for years, a smile shrouded by an invisible aura of mystery; the beautiful, big-breasted blonde was my Mona Lisa. What was she smiling about? I wanted to know.

Maybe Mary knew.

She knew everything a little girl was not supposed to.

This wasn't her first time watching the video. She'd watched it with her dad. She knew what was going to happen next. She had it memorized like she had every line from Beauty and the Beast in her memory.

All the while as we watched the video, I would see her from time to time glancing at me in the corner of my eye as if she were more interested in how I was reacting to the video than the video itself. When I sensed her looking at me I felt something almost imperceptible pass between us, something I had no name for, something that left me and entered her, as something in her walked out her body into mine.

A little piece of Mary inside me.

As she watched me watching the video it felt as if she were in my head feeling what I felt; all the emotions she could no longer feel she felt again vicariously through me. It was the old Mary I remembered from before, getting high off my innocence as she snorted it from my body. And I thought I could feel what Mary felt as she viewed the video once again that she'd seen so many times with her dad. I felt it as a vacancy inside me. It was a feeling of not feeling.

A strange numbness.

An emptiness.

That was the vibe Mary gave off.

I could feel her emptiness being filled by my shock as I gazed in transfixed wonder at the TV screen where the beautiful blond with big boobies was screaming out as if she were in horrible pain as she gripped one man's cock tightly in her left hand while the other two men violently rammed their cocks into her, one man crushing her from above as he stabbed his cock into her pussy, while the other man was beneath her piercing her sphincter with his cock, his arms reaching from around her back to where he gripped onto her bulging breasts, squeezing them hard without an ounce of gentleness, slapping them again and again until her breasts glowed red, and sadistically twisting her nipples. The woman was suffering. It was obvious. Her face was twisted into a grimace as she let out a series of squeaking noises that sounded inhuman like some wounded animal. The two men seemed to be squeezing the life out of her, and they seemed to know this, and it was as if they didn't care, they just continued battering into her with their cocks, each man pulling at her from one side, as if they were trying to split her in half.

That seemed to be the point.

To tear her apart, rip her to pieces.

The woman continued to scream in torment.

She let out a loud high-pitched wailing sound that hurt my ears. I couldn't watch anymore. They were going to kill her. I closed my eyes but I still saw it. The video was playing in my head as the sounds I heard from the video painted images in my mind even more grotesque than the ones I'd seen on the TV screen. I plugged up my ears with my two index fingers to cut my imagination off from the sounds that were twisting it into a vision of terror, but I still could hear; she was screaming so loudly, in such a tortured voice, like a damned soul crying up from hell. I couldn't take it anymore. I told my body to get up and run from the room, but my body wouldn't listen to me. I felt tears rushing to fill my eyes. I wanted to scream. Scream what I was feeling out of me.

Scream her scream out of my head.

Then she stopped screaming for just a moment and spoke. "Yeah. Just like that. Oh! That feels so fucking good," she said. As soon as the last word left her lips she began shouting a painful sound again that was one long drawn out scream interrupted every few seconds with her saying something like "Fuck yeah" or "Just like that" or "That feels so fucking good."

This sent a mixed message that expanded the cognitive dissonance the video had brought into my mind. I was thinking one thought with its opposite, an irreconcilable contradiction: the woman in my head, my eyes closed but still seeing, hearing her screaming out in torment as she encouraged her tormenters to torment her some more, crying out how good she felt right before she began crying like a person being beaten to death, punctuating this cry of torment by saying, "Fuck yeah, just like that."

My eyes were still closed.

But I saw what I heard.

The woman in my mind, my confusion, the mystery behind her image, something I could not yet fathom. What was she feeling? Pleasure or pain? Maybe both at the same time, pain merged into pleasure. Could there be such a thing? How could something be what it was and wasn't at the same time? How could something be its opposite?

All I knew was that I didn't know.

I was six years old.

The woman continued to moan, but it no longer sounded like she was in pain to me. It had become a sound vacant of meaning that was at the same time not meaningless. What her cries had meant to me at first had been stolen by the words she spoke, exalting what the men were doing to her. Her cry was the sound representing my confusion, an enigma, an emptiness filling with my curiosity. That's what the woman's voice became in my head, a shocking, pleasure-filled terror that wasn't what it was or appeared to be, but was something else entirely: a mystery.

Her moaning began to break into intervals stretched between the words fuck yes: moan fuck yes moan fuck yes moan. To my six-year-old ears fuck was the worst word in existence. I had heard people use it before but only at the worst moments. I'd heard my mom say it once. She tripped down the stairs and sprained her ankle and said, "Oh, fuck," when she'd reached the bottom. Once at a baseball game a drunk guy in the stands yelled, "Fuck you," to the umpire and he had to be escorted out of the stadium afterwards as a penalty. A kid in my class said he didn't give a fuck about something and the kid he'd said it to told on him and he had to go to the principal's office where he was forced to call his mom at her work place and tell her what he'd said in class while the principal stood over him. But what did the word fuck mean?

Its meaning was hidden behind its sound where I could not see it.

It was a secret.

Something I wasn't supposed to know, like what I was seeing in the video.

"You're going to miss the ending," said Mary right then, "Open your eyes, sweetie pie. It's OK. The ending is the best part. I promise."

Mary had called me sweetie pie. That was strange. She'd never said that to me before. It was like she was not herself talking to someone not me. But the words sweetie pie had a charming ring in my ears. It sounded like something you said to someone you loved, or that's how it sounded when Mary said it to me; and at that moment, I felt a sisterly bond to her that I still cannot explain to this day. Her words repeated themselves in my thoughts: The ending is the best part, I promise, the best part, it's OK, sweetie pie, I promise.

I opened my eyes.

For Mary.

And the part of me that wanted to see.

What I saw was the weirdest thing of all, the most bizarre thing I'd ever seen. The men pulled their cocks out of all the woman's holes as they stroked themselves rapidly while standing over her until white goo began to shoot out of the little holes at the end of their cocks onto the woman's body. I thought they were peeing on her, but their pee was thick and white for some strange reason unknown to me. They covered her whole body with the stuff. One guy did it all over her breasts then rubbed the head of his cock around where he'd ejaculated, spreading the strange white goo with the end of his cock into a thin layer all over her boobs, making them look greasy, laminated in a glossy sheen. Another guy shot his white stuff all in her beautiful blond hair. It seemed so demeaning. What could possibly be the purpose of doing something like that? I hadn't a clue. But where the third guy spread his white goo on the woman seemed just as senseless. He did it on her face. A lot of it came out of him, more than had come out of all the other guys, and he

101

shot it everywhere on her face, splattering some of it in her right eye, getting some of it on her forehead, her cheek, in her left ear, and all across her lips. The guy who did this to her face was the same guy who had closed her nostrils shut while smothering her with his cock.

The camera did a close up of her face. She looked different than when I'd first seen her, changed somehow, less beautiful, disfigured. Her makeup was running down her face in a mess, all smeared together with the goo and the tears she'd cried; there were sharp lines cutting across her face from the way she was wincing, wincing because of her right eye, where the one guy had peed his white goo into; it was squeezed tightly shut, covered in a slimy white film, twitching constantly as if irritated. I wondered if her eye stung like mine did when ever shampoo got into it while I was showering. The goo on her forehead had begun to snail a trail down the bridge of her nose, while the goo on her cheek had slimed its way to the edge of her jaw, where a lumpy strand of it dangled, looking like it was about to drop down to her breasts to mix with the goo left there by the other guy; her left ear just looked gross, like it had some kind of white fungus growing out of it, and clumps of her once beautiful blond hair were matted together in a gooey tangle. Her lips were closed as if sealed shut by the goo the guy had put there with his cock. She wasn't smiling like she had been before when she was down on her knees gobbling on the men's cocks when the video had first begun. She had looked proud then. Confident. Now she looked slightly embarrassed as if she were humiliated, completely drenched in the gooey white liquid.

"What is that stuff?" I asked Mary.

"Cum," said Mary.

"What's cum?" I asked.

"Cum's the stuff babies are made from," Mary said.

"How?" I asked.

"The man has to put it inside the woman to make a baby," she said. "That's why they put it outside her, because they don't want to make a baby with her."

"Oh. OK," I said. It was a good enough explanation, I guess, but it didn't really explain the point of putting it on her face or in her hair or in her eye or everywhere else they'd put it on her body.

"Why did they do it on her face?" I asked Mary.

"Because it feels good," she said.

Feels good for who? I wondered. For the man or the woman or both? How did that stuff, what I'd just learned was called cum, how did it feel on her skin? And how did Mary know? How did she know it felt good?

Where had she learned that?

My wondering was intruded upon by a voice from the TV speaking to the woman from behind the camera. "Smile for the camera, slut," and the woman did what the voice told her to do. She smiled, her cum-covered lips like an oozing white slug squirming into a curl. Then the voice asked her, "How does it feel to be fucked by three guys, slut?"

Was that what fuck meant? I wondered. Was it the word for what the three guys had done to the woman with their cocks? If that was true, I wondered, then what did that have to do with my mom spraining her ankle? Why would she say that? What did spraining her ankle have to do with what cocks did to a woman?

As I thought about all this, the woman answered the question, saying, "Really, really fucking fantastic," and as her lips parted while she spoke, strands of cum like silk from a spider web stretched out between her lips, looking disgusting to me, and then when she'd finished talking she licked the cum off her lips with her tongue and said, "Yum."

This made me wonder: did the stuff men peed from their cocks, the stuff called cum, the stuff that turned into a baby when it got inside a woman, did it taste good? What did it taste like?

"Do you like the taste of cum?" the voice asked the woman.

"Yes," said the woman.

"You're a little slut, aren't you," asked the voice.

"Yeah. I'm a slut," she answered.

Then the video image got all distorted like before. The cum-drenched, beautiful, big-breasted blond broke apart into a scramble as the TV screen became hazy until all there was to see was a mishmash of static; but then suddenly the distortion disappeared as an image of two naked woman in bed together came into view. One woman had her face buried in the other woman's vagina, who was moaning loudly in response to whatever the woman was doing to her down there. So loudly, that I didn't hear the doorbell ring, or the front door open, or hear the footsteps in the hallway outside the room. I didn't hear anything but the sounds coming from the video.

Until the door opened and my mom walked in.

The noises coming from the TV must have alerted her instantly that we were not watching something made by Disney, and as her eyes landed on the bright pornographic images shining from the television, she gasped loudly and shouted, "Lisa! Oh my Lord! What are you girls watching?"

And that's how I learned what sex was.

A Skipping CD

The morning after the angels had witnessed me masturbating, when I had learned that the devil wanted me to be his wife and to impregnate me with the Antichrist, I was not woken up by my mother like usual but by my grandmother instead. The interesting thing was that my grandmother had been dead for over seven years.

I was slowly tugged out from my dreams by a soft feminine voice saying, "Rise and shine, sunshine." I thought it was my mother at first, but she hadn't woken me up with those words since I was a little girl. "I used to say it to her, too, when she was little," said the voice as if responding to what I'd just thought.

I sat up in bed and looked about my room that was the color of the dawn peeking through the window. The voice had responded to my thoughts, it seemed, so it couldn't be my mother; only the angels responded to what I thought, but all their voices had been male sounding up until that point. So, then, who had it been? I replayed in my mind what the voice had said to me. That's when it hit me. I realized who the voice was coming from.

Could it be? I thought. Was it her?

"Grandmother?" I asked out loud.

"It's me, baby. I've missed you so much."

I couldn't believe it. I was really talking to my dead grandmother. "Are you an angel now?" I asked her.

"Yes, sweetie," she said, "I'm up in heaven where you'll be one day, if the devil doesn't win."

"I want God to win, Grandmother," I said.

"He will," she responded, "As long as you never do what you did last night again."

As her words sank in they burst into a feeling of extreme shame and embarrassment. Not only had God and the angels and Satan and his demons seen what I had done, but my grandmother had seen me play with my vagina, too.

All privacy was gone.

"I promise I'll never do it again," I said to my grandmother as the door to my room opened and my mom walked in.

When her eyes fell on me sitting up in bed, she said, "Oh, you're already up. Who were you talking to just now, the tooth fairy?"

"Uh, I was talking in my sleep," I said to my mother in a stammer.

"Lying is a sin," I heard an angel say.

"I'm sorry," I said to the angel, but my mom thought I was talking to her. She said, "What are you sorry for? Talking in your sleep isn't a sin."

"Oh. I don't know. I mean. Yeah. You're right," I said, trying to swallow the words I don't know because I did know, I had known what I meant by saying sorry, and saying I didn't was a lie; I was trying to cover my sin before it had a chance to sink into my skin and become an awful feeling, but I was too late, the angels saw my sin before I did, and I could feel them carrying God's judgment into me.

"All right, then," said my mother, "breakfast is on the table."

At breakfast, the two lies I had already told before the day had barely begun stayed with me in the form of a heavy feeling over my chest, where what I had done the night before was also clenching my heart in its black fist, its blackness staining my heart, which then began to pump its new color into the rest of my body. I wanted to make it all go away through confession, but not to God; I wanted to confess to my mom. I wanted to tell her everything. Tell her all about the angels, about being a prophet, about being stuck in the middle of a battle, where God was fighting the devil for my soul the devil, who wanted to wed me then make me give birth to his child. I wanted to tell my mother all this and also tell her that I had just spoken to her mother, my grandmother, before she had walked into my room and interrupted our conversation. It all sounded crazy, but it was all true, though it probably wouldn't sound like truth in my mother's ears. It would sound like insanity. Even so, I was possessed by an urge so strong, an urge to tell her all about everything that I had been through in the past couple of weeks. But I didn't even know how to begin to tell her what I wanted to tell her, and as I thought about all this,

I heard an angel say, "If you tell her, Satan, will come after her, too."

The angel's comment added yet another dimension to the newly developed reality the angels had brought with them when they first entered my life. What the angel had just said meant my family could be in put in harm's way if I told them anything. This new revelation, I realized, also meant that anyone I told about all this could become threatened by Satan as well. Anyone I confided in about what was happening to me would then be introduced to the evil force that was attempting to have its way with me, placing them in the same danger I was in. So, even if I could muster up the courage to tell my mother about the angels, and figure out the right way to tell her, it was something I couldn't do. This new fact meant I was trapped in this world of mine, because this world was not something I could share with anybody else.

While I was reflecting on what the angel had made known to me just then, the reality of the situation suddenly became very clear to me; I was hermetically sealed in this world of angels and demons by the silence I had to keep about it in order to protect my loved ones from Satan and his hoard of demonic angels.

I felt so alone as I thought about Satan in my head.

And as I thought these thoughts an angel (or demon) shouted, "He wants you for his wife!"

Satan wanted to marry me.

The angel or demon, whichever it was, had said so last night, and now it had said it again, reinforcing what I had felt when I'd heard it the first time, making the threat appear even more ominous and real.

Was he watching me now? I wondered: were the devil's eyes on me at that very moment?

"Yes," said an angel either from above or below, "he's always watching you."

Like God, I thought, always watching me, and there was nowhere I could hide where he would not see me. This revelation cast a dark shadow over my world, the world that was not the world of my mother and father, or Steph and Julie, or anyone else, but my own little private world; and the longer I lived in it, the further I felt myself drifting away from the planet I once shared with everyone I knew. It was this morning that I first began to develop the sense that I was now traveling in a direction opposite to where everyone else was heading. I wanted to return to them. Live on their planet once again. Follow them. Go where they were going.

This was a change from what I'd felt before. Hearing angels at first had been exciting, but then the devil and his angels the night before had joined the heavenly choir I'd grown fond of; and now I wanted no part of it, I no longer wanted to hear angels anymore, good or bad. I just wanted to hear what everyone else heard. That was what made me like them, I thought, hearing what they also heard; and now that I had heard what they could not, it was like I wasn't even the same species as them. I was an alien.

"It's your cross to bear," said an angel.

"You're a prophet," said another.

I'm a prophet, I thought, and Satan's after me.

"He wants you for his wife!" an angel shouted, repeating what had just been said moments ago, repeating what had been said the night before quite a few times, repeating what would be repeated again and again through out the rest of the day, each time a thought of the devil popped into my mind.

I didn't like this. I wanted it all to go away.

The first time after the angels had come they had been gone for almost a week before they returned, a week where I waited for them to come back in eager anticipation; and then after they came the second time they had been gone for about another week and had not returned until the moment after my orgasm ended the night before. This time, they were still there, the morning after, and I didn't want them to be. I wanted them to leave like they had before and never come back again. But it was out of my control, I knew this, and I had no idea what I could do.

Usually when I had a problem I couldn't handle on my own I went to my mother. As I was thinking about my mom an angel repeated, "If you tell her, Satan will come after her, too," and it made me think again about how he was after me, and thinking this led to an angel reminding me once again of the devil's intentions, reminding me in a screaming shout, "He wants you for his wife!"

All this repetition was beginning to get to me.

I was starting to recognize a pattern between what I thought and what the angels said. They were starting to seem as repetitive in what they said as the thoughts caused by what they said, thoughts that circled round and round in an obsessive whirl, triggering the same phrases from the angels again and again every time I thought them. How did this feel? I didn't know quite how to describe it, but the image of a dog chasing its own tail came to mind.

As I sat at the table I continued to think the same thoughts that I'd first begun thinking the night before, and the angels and demons responded to these thoughts with the same phrases they'd used before when I'd thought the same thing. I wanted to stop hearing what the angels were saying again and again in response to what I was thinking, and I wanted to stop thinking the thoughts that made the angels say what I didn't want to hear them say. But how could I do this? It was a problem with no obvious solution.

Who could I turn to?

"Pray," said an angel at the same time my mother said, "Eat, Lisa."

I hadn't touched my food. It was cereal. I took the spoon I'd been gripping tightly in my hand and dipped it into the bowl as I thought the word pray over and over as an angel repeated what I thought the moment I thought it, so the thought pray in my head also became a sound in my ears.

Pray. Hearing this word, thinking it in my mind, made it clear to me: God was the only one I could turn to now. I began to shovel the cereal into my mouth as I prayed thoughts an angel vocalized out loud in a sound I could hear fill the kitchen. My mother was oblivious to this noise even though she was sitting across from me reading the newspaper. The angel's voice seemed to cut an invisible line between my mother and me, forming a wall of separation neither of us could cross.

I continued to eat my cereal as I finished my prayer to God, asking Him to protect me from the devil and watch over me and my family, a prayer I had prayed many times now, a prayer that was becoming routine, a litany, that seemed to lose some of its meaning each time I repeated

113

it to God in my thoughts. As I took my last bite of food, I said amen in my head then got up to dump the remaining cereal floating in a pool of milk down the garbage disposal before I put the emptied bowl in the dishwasher. Then I made my way to the bathroom to take my shower.

While in the shower I thought about my grandmother.

Was she still watching me? Observing me as I washed my naked body?

"Grandmother?" I asked in a voice I heard echo back to me off the bathroom walls. I waited to hear her voice, but my grandmother didn't answer back. However, an angel did, saying, "She's with God now, but she's always watching you."

"Will she be back to talk with me?" I asked the angel as I soaped my breasts, feeling a bit embarrassed that I was being watched by my grandmother, the angels, and God knows what other dead relatives as I did this.

"Soon," the angel answered me.

This brightened my mood some. I wanted to communicate with my grandmother some more, and I was glad I would have the opportunity to do it again, soon, as the angel had said. Even if I couldn't tell my mother I had talked to her mother, I hoped, maybe somehow, I could deliver messages to my mom from her mom without revealing the source these messages were coming from.

Trying to figure out how I could do this without having to make something up, I continued to wash my naked body. I had never felt so naked in my life. Nobody had ever seen me naked but me, or so I'd thought, and being watched right then made me feel self-conscious. I didn't like how my body looked. What I saw in the mirror was something I wanted to alter completely. My hips were too wide, so were my thighs, and my boobs were much bigger than I wanted them to be, way too big for my body. I thought they made me look fat, and I always felt them hanging there like a heavy weight, a nuisance.

They hurt my body and caused me back pain.

Julie often commented that she wished she had my boobs instead of hers, and I would have gladly traded her because hers were slender and perky and fit her body perfectly, unlike mine, which I tried to shrink, by squeezing them behind a sports bra I usually wore in place of a regular one. My nipples often stuck through my bra, rising up in an indention quite visible through my shirt, and whenever Julie would noticed this, almost always, she would say, "Is it cold in here or is it just you?" Every time after I first heard her say this, every time I heard someone ask me, "Isn't it cold in here?" especially when it was a boy who'd asked me this, a part of me would wonder if they were referring to my hard nipples in a subtle way.

When Julie talked about wanting my boobs to be hers she seemed to desire them because she thought that the boys at our school desired them also. Once Julie told me that whenever she was walking with me in the halls at school, she would catch guys staring down at my chest all the time. But I never noticed this, and I responded to what she said with surprise, and she told me I was so naive. After this I would try to catch guys looking at my boobs, but every time I looked at a guy I thought was looking at me, he would quickly look away, as if my face repelled him, and I never got a chance to see which part of me he was looking at, if any. And I wondered every time I heard a rumor that a certain boy liked me if it was just because of my boobs that Julie made such a big deal about. I didn't want my boobs to be the reason a guy liked me.

My boobs weren't quite as big as the woman from the video, but almost:, and when Julie said what she said to me, it made me wonder if boys waned to do to my breasts what the guys in the porno had done to the woman's? Did they want to slap them, twist my nipples, suck on them, and squeeze them hard between their hands? Sometimes I wondered what it would feel like, wondered what my breasts would feel like in a guy's hands—another guilt-laden desire, another feeling I felt that I didn't want to feel. I knew from touching them myself that the tips of my nipples were sensitive; they felt good to touch at certain times, and they stung when I twisted them, but in a good way, I couldn't quite explain, as long as I didn't do it too hard and twisted them just right.

Just as I was washing the soap off my breasts I thought about the devil again for some reason.

"He wants you for his wife!" the angel shouted.

Was it because of my boobs? Was that why the devil wanted to marry me?

"He wants you to have his child," said an angel, again saying what had been said before, and what would be said again the next time I thought again about how the devil wanted to marry me.

Maybe if my boobs were smaller, I thought, he would want to impregnate another girl with the Antichrist instead of me. Maybe if Julie had gotten her wish and my boobs had become hers, the devil would have come after her and not me.

As the water washed the soapsuds off my breasts it hit directly against my nipples in a concentrated spray, which then made them tingle, tingle with a sensation I found pleasing, and something began stirring in my vagina, as if the sensation in my nipples were communicating what they were feeling down to it. I instantly associated what was going on down there as sexual, so I turned my breasts quickly away the spray of water, feeling a tinge of guilt as I did this because I'd liked the way it felt.

The next part of the shower was the worst. My hair had been washed and so had everywhere else on my body, excluding one area, my vagina. I had been avoiding it the whole time, but I had to wash it. It felt gross; it always did the day after, the day after any night like the night before, when I did what I'd done then—my terrible sin. And as I scrubbed it clean, my vagina, I couldn't help but think about the way I'd touched it before. I thought about Patrick. How he had been my husband, then a stranger, then a rapist, and as I thought about this, thought about what I'd been thinking the night before and what I had done while I'd been thinking this, one angel said, "Never do that again," right as another one asked, "Lisa, are you a little slut?" so the words of these two angels, one from God, the other from Satan, overlapped in my ears into a twisted knot, a knot that unraveled in my mind, where I thought about each phrase separately, simultaneously.

I responded to the good angel first, saying, "I wont. I promise," just as I had promised the angels and God so many times already since the night before. Then I addressed myself to the demonic angel, proclaiming, "No. I am not a slut."

"Then why are you touching your pussy?" it said.

"Because it has to be cleaned," I said.

"Why does it have to be cleaned?" it asked.

"It just does!" I said.

"Don't lie. You know what you did. You're a little slut," the evil angel said.

"No I'm not!" I almost shouted.

"Then why did you do it?" the demon asked.

I didn't know what to say or how to say it. What I had done last night was in my head something a slut did, and so a section of my psyche believed what the demonic angel said, and this part of me answered: yes, I am a slut, silently in my thoughts, as a stronger part of my mind moved forth to dominate this thought, smacking it back down into the darkness. This larger part of me proclaimed that I was a good person, not a slut.

"I bet you want to play with it again," the demonic angel said.

"No!" I said. I washed my vagina as fast as I could. Then I turned off the water, stepped out of the shower, toweled off, and covered my body in the clothes I'd picked out for that day, getting dressed as quickly as I possibly could, hoping to feel more secure somehow, less visible; but I still felt naked, imagining that the ones who could see past my skull into my brain could also see through my clothing as well.

That's how I felt all day: naked. Naked with no way to cover up as the angels, good and bad, continued to respond to my thoughts. Thinking became less like thinking and more like one long conversation I did not want to have. And the only way to end this conversation, since I couldn't quiet the angels, was to stop thinking. But I couldn't, and every time I tried to silence my thoughts, they overpowered my efforts and continued to fountain up into my awareness in a never-ending stream.

On the bus ride to school I was quiet, even quieter than my old self, and I just sat there while Steph and Julie gabbed while my attention was mostly absorbed by the ongoing conversation with the angels I was having inside my head. I kept thinking the same thoughts and they kept saying the same things. I would think about what I had done and an angel would tell me to never do that again, again, which would make me think about what I had done some more, as an angel would tell me what it had told me the night before about the nature of my fantasy, saying, "That wasn't Patrick, that was the devil"; and when the angel said this I would think of the devil, and when I thought of the devil, an angel would remind me what I kept being reminded of, telling me that the devil wanted me for his wife, and when I heard this I would then think about how he wanted me to give birth to his child, and an angel would confirm this thought by repeating what had been said before, informing me that the devil did indeed want me to have his child.

This exchange between my thoughts and the angels repeated itself one time after the other on the whole way to school where this looping thought spiral continued to twist its way through my day. There on the bus, for the very first time, I tried to ignore the angels and made my best attempt to listen to my friends while I searched for a way to contribute in some way to what they were talking about. They were talking about ordinary stuff, but as I followed their back and forth, I realized they were conversing about a world I no longer shared with them. I couldn't relate to them anymore. I was different from them now. They didn't talk to angels or their dead grandmothers. I was separated from them, too, surrounded by an impenetrable boundary; the wall between my mother and me that I had perceived at breakfast that morning had stretched out to connect with a wall separating me from Steph and Julie. They were on the other side with my mom, where my dad and sister were also, along with everyone else who didn't hear what I did.

I wanted to smash through the wall and tell Steph and Julie about everything, but as I wished for this, an angel said, "Tell them and Satan will come after them, too," which pounded into me what I had intuited already earlier that morning, the awful realization that the same rule about being unable to confide to my mother about the angels also applied to my two best friends and, I assumed, to anybody who wasn't an angel or God.

And what did it matter?

Even if I could tell them they wouldn't believe me. They would think I was nuts. But I wasn't nuts. Was I? Or maybe I was. I considered this, but as I did, the angels continued to talk to me, their voices making a sound, which was no more or less real sounding than the voices I heard coming out of my friends' mouths along with the chatter coming from the other kids on the bus. No, I wasn't crazy, I told myself, this was really happening.

But why didn't anyone else hear what I heard?

I had wondered this before and now I wondered it again.

"You're a prophet," an angel said. It was the same thing an angel had said before when I had asked myself the same question. Hearing it again made it no longer seem like an answer at all but just a series of enigmatic words instead, which only produced more questions. OK, I am a prophet, so that's why I can hear angels, I thought, but why am I a prophet? I asked the angels in my head. They hadn't answered that yet. Impatient for a response, I repeated this question again and again in my mind—what makes me a prophet...what makes me a prophet...what makes me a prophet—not ending this repeating thought sequence until I finally received an answer of some kind from the angels. But when it came it wasn't the answer I was looking for.

An angel said, "God does."

Hearing this only frustrated me some more. It was like what my parents had always said in response to almost all my questions about the world when I was a little girl: because of God, because of God, because of God.

What made me a prophet? God did. That's what the angel said. I felt anger towards it. I wanted to say, "Well, duh." Of course, God made me a prophet. That was something I already knew. Everyone was the way they were because God made them that way, but what I really wanted to know was why God had made me this way, why had God chosen me to be a prophet, and I asked the angels this with my mind, asking why, why, why, until an angel said, "Because He wants you to deliver a message from Him to the world."

This told me nothing new. I'd already heard this. The angels were just repeating what they'd said before when I had asked basically the same questions. Why were they so repetitious? It was like they had a limited stock of phrases they could say like a trained parrot or a talking programmed robot. Why didn't they answer my real question with a real answer? Why didn't they tell me why? Were they just toying with my mind? Which angels were talking to me, I also wondered, God's, or Satan's? As I wondered this two voices said, "Yes," not quite in unison so one yes ended and began just before and after the other yes was said.

It was like they were messing with my head.

But why?

Why? Why? Why?

Why does God want me to deliver a message to the world? I asked. Why me, why not someone else, why did He choose me to be his prophet, please, please just tell me why.

"The Lord works in mysterious ways," an angel answered.

This answer only frustrated me some more. It was also something they had said before. And it was the same thing my parents had always said, which never really seemed like an answer to my question but more like a sort of remedy for it, as if what I was wondering was an ailment the words, "God works in mysterious ways" could somehow cure.

All this told me was that there were some things I could never know. It was what God knew that I couldn't. He kept certain things secret from you, I came to believe, until you died and went to heaven (if you got in), where you learned the answer to every question—learned why God did what He did.

I didn't want to hear this from the angels. I knew the Lord worked in mysterious ways. I had heard that all my life. Why couldn't they just tell me why God had chosen me? Why keep it a secret?

Tell me, I said in my head, tell me why. Why, why, why?

"Lisa," said Steph, "is something wrong?"

Hearing her brought me back into the bus as if I had been somewhere else all along. Not wanting to lie, I said, "Kind of."

"What?" she asked.

"It's hard to explain," I said.

"Well, you're being so quiet," she said. "What are you thinking about?"

"Yeah," said Julie. "What's on your mind?"

"If I told you, your souls would be in danger of eternal damnation," I said.

"Uh. OK," said Julie. "Lisa, you're so weird sometimes. It's like you live on another planet. I swear."

"Why would we be in that kind of danger if you told us?" Steph asked.

"I don't know," I said, and I wasn't telling a lie. I really didn't know why the devil would come after them if I told them about the angels.

"Then what are you talking about?" asked Julie.

"I wish I could tell you, but I cant," I said.

"Secrets don't make friends," she responded.

I wanted someway to take the attention off me, but I couldn't think of anything to say except "Sorry."

"Whatever," Julie said. And then, to my relief, she and Steph moved on to other things. I remained quiet for the rest of the bus ride as they talked to one another like I wasn't there, and I wasn't there, not really. I was somewhere else, with the angels, in a place where my friends could not go, on the other side of the wall.

The wall...

The wall crisscrossed its way through my day, connecting end to end, dividing me from everybody, forming a maze around where I went, a maze I was within that was within me, something outside me yet inside me, something all around me that was also in my head; a maze I wandered in, a maze my thoughts circulated through as I tried to think my way out from it.

Every exit was an entrance into another maze exactly the same as the one I had just found my way out of. I was moving in the direction the angels were guiding me in. The good angels pointed right while the bad ones pointed left. I tried to listen to the good angels only, to move towards where the glorious vision they had put in my head became reality, as I tried to steer away from the path that led to where the vision the bad angels had painted in my head came true; but sometimes I got confused which angels were from God and which were from Satan. I didn't know which way to turn next as my thoughts clashed, moving in opposing directions.

As the day continued, the angels stayed with me constantly, saying the same things over and over again in response to the thoughts I couldn't stop thinking. How many times have I already said this? How many times have I told you that the angels kept saying the same exact things in response to the same exact thoughts I couldn't stop thinking? Am I beginning to sound repetitious? Well, if that's the case, maybe you can now get an inkling of what I was going through as I heard the same thing from moment to moment, where one moment began to resemble the next, where the scenery was always the same even when I went somewhere else, because I didn't go anywhere I went that day, nowhere but where I remained, locked in my head with the angels and demons, as the outside world passed by without leaving much of an impression.

In math class I tried to ignore them and concentrate on taking notes as I attempted to focus on the teacher's lecture. It's hard to ignore something that can see into your head. The angels said something about almost every one of my thoughts, which made me think about what they said, which then made them say something about what I thought about what they said.

When would the angels go away again? I wondered.

Would they always be with me?

"For eternity," said an angel.

An eternity? I asked.

"Yes," said an angel.

Where, I asked, heaven or hell?

"Heaven," said a good angel as a bad one said, "Hell," so the two words merged into one as I heard them spoken in unison, leaving me confused. Didn't God already know? I wondered. Didn't He know everything? Didn't He know if I was going to have the devil's baby or not?

"He knows He will win and you will become his prophet," a good angel said at the same time a bad one said, "He knows you're going to have the devil's child." What the two angels said garbled into one sound as their contradictory words clashed against one another in my ears, but somehow I made out what they'd both said. My mind was being divided by the angels and demons, pulled in two directions.

I wanted to believe the good angel over the bad one.

The devil lies, I told myself. That's what I'd always heard.

"That's true," said an angel.

I had stopped taking notes and had ceased listening to my teacher. I had missed the whole lesson, and we were going to have a quiz over the material covered in it on Wednesday that week. I would have to go to after-school tutoring to catch up, I told myself as the bell rang.

I got up out from my desk and followed behind a line of my classmates into the congested hallway crowded with students. The students had ordered their collective movement into two-way traffic. I pushed my way through the students heading away from where I needed to go until I crossed over into the flow of students moving towards where my next class was located. My next class was Advanced English, my favorite subject and usually my favorite part of the school day; but as I got closer and closer to my destination a growing sense of dread expanded out in front me as I made my way to where he would be.

Patrick.

He was in my next class.

I tried to decrease my speed, not wanting to get where I was going fast, but the mass of students behind me forced me to keep up with the pace of the foot traffic. When I passed the F-Hall bathroom, without thinking or knowing why I departed from the row of students and made my way to the bathroom door, which a girl in front of me opened. I followed her in. I was not compelled into the bathroom by any bodily urges. It was something else. I was avoiding going to English class, delaying the inevitable, because I would have to go eventually since skipping it was out of the question. I had never skipped a class in my life. To me, it was impossible, something I was sure I would never let myself do.

While in the F-Hall bathroom I felt like I was somewhere I shouldn't be. It had a bad reputation as the bathroom all the bad kids would go to when they wanted to smoke a cigarette or something even worse, like pot, or God knows what. I had never actually been in the F-Hall bathroom before, and when I walked in, there was a crowd of girls gathered around the sinks in front of the mirrors, smoking cigarettes. They all looked up at me simultaneously as if they were a single entity. I imagined they were all thinking the same thing while they stared at me: what is she doing here? It was the same question I asked myself as I hid from their eyes inside a bathroom stall, where I began to think about him, and him: the devil and Patrick, Patrick, whom I couldn't think about without remembering how the devil had raped me in my head after Trojan horsing into my mind hidden within a sexual fantasy about Patrick.

As soon as Satan returned to my thoughts my mind became completely dominated by them. These thoughts felt alive, intruders, a presence I could feel occupying my head, as if these thoughts about him, the devil, were actually him, within me. Standing there in the bathroom stall everything I was hearing outside it began to remind me of him somehow. It was mostly the girls outside the stall smoking cigarettes. Their words turned into thoughts of the devil. It began to feel like the devil was talking to me somehow through their voices. As if he had control over them and they didn't know it. They were smokers and they talked about bad stuff. They were sinners, well, so was I, but it was like they were proud of their sins, as if they had chosen to side with the devil; that's how I perceived them right then. They were the girls who dressed all in black and wore Marilyn Manson T-shirts. They listened to evil music that insulted God and exalted the devil. Everything they said was somehow associated in my mind with sin.

Then it got more intense. One of the girls was talking about how she'd been "freaking out" all last week because she'd thought she was pregnant, "but then I got my period this morning," she told the other girls, "and I was like fucking thank you Jesus Christ!"

She was a tool in the hand of the devil.

That what I thought right then.

She was a ventriloquist dummy on his lap saying words that put thoughts of him into my head. That's what it seemed like to me. Hearing about pregnancy inevitably made me think once again about how the devil wanted to make me pregnant with his offspring. Then these thoughts shaped into a question I hadn't asked myself yet: how would he try to impregnate me? I knew how the girl talking outside the stall I was in had almost gotten pregnant: she'd had sex with some guy.

I wondered, would the devil have to have sex with me to put his wicked seed in my womb or could he do it through other means? Wondering this made me think about something that had always been a mystery to me: the mystery of how God impregnated Mary with Jesus Christ. Which meant he impregnated Mary with himself, because Jesus was God in the flesh. But how exactly did God do this? It didn't say anywhere in the Bible that God came down to earth and had sex with Mary. And such a thing would have been out of the question, because Mary was about to marry Joseph, and she was much too pure to ever cheat on him, even if it was God Himself who was attempting to seduce her. So, since God didn't impregnate her through physical intercourse, then He must've done it some other way. I'd always imagined He'd magically thought his seed into Mary somehow. This was something God could do. He could do anything He wanted to. He was all-powerful. Anytime He wanted to make a change in reality He could do it without barely lifting a finger.

Nothing was impossible to God.

But what about Satan?

Could he think his seed into me?

Intuitively I somehow knew this was not within his abilities. This meant that we would have to have sex. And if he could come to me in the form of an erotic fantasy where he raped me, he might be able to cross into reality and rape me for real this time. What would he look like when he came to do this to me? Would I recognize him? He had appeared in my head in the guise of Patrick and then effortlessly changed into a completely different person when he began to rape me in the fantasy. If he could be anyone in my fantasies, then maybe he could take any shape he desired when he came up to Earth from hell in his physical form. He could come to me disguised as anyone. Maybe he already had, I thought. Maybe he was hidden within the skin of someone I knew, or thought I knew, who was waiting for the perfect opportunity to seduce me with his devilish charm; and then when I resisted, he would take me by force. What would I do then? I didn't believe in abortion, but if the fetus in me were the Antichrist, I would have to get one for the good of humanity. But the devil must know that I would do this. Satan is crafty, I realized, and was probably already steps ahead of me, planning what he would do next based on his predictions of what I would do next to keep my soul from becoming his, setting traps designed to ensnare me in sinfulness today that were set to go off tomorrow and trying to think of a way to surprise me, to trick me.

The whole time I was pondering the devil and how he would get me pregnant, some angels, or maybe they were demons, kept shouting over and over, "He wants you for his wife!" Not just one of them, but many of them, some saying it at the same time, others speaking out of step, like an out-of-tune choir singing one hymn again and again: "He wants you for his wife, he wants you for his wife, he wants you for his wife." Their words trampled over one another as their voices intermingled with the ones coming from the girls smoking outside, while my thoughts swirled like the water in the flushing toilets I heard in the stalls next to mine as they spiraled their way down to a fearful conclusion. I was so caught up in what I was thinking that I didn't really hear the angels even though I did, but as I came to what seemed like a dead end where my train of thought halted I heard what I'd been hearing over and over like I was hearing it for the first time: the devil wants you for his wife.

The devil wants me…

…for his wife.

He wants to marry me.

Would this be how he'd come?

In the form of my husband?

Not some random acquaintance who would find some way to get close to me so he could take my virginity one night against my will, but instead, the devil would appear to me as the guy I would eventually marry. I would spend the rest of my life with him thinking he was someone he was not. We would start a family together and I wouldn't know our child was the Antichrist. I would raise and nurture him, and, when he came of age, using the charisma he'd inherited from his trickster father, he would climb his way up through the ranks of politics, rising to a position of power, where he'd execute the devil's master plan. The world would become Satan's domain. The beginning of the end would begin.

The apocalypse.

I saw it all so clearly in my head.

"You're a prophet," an angel said, and when it did, it gave this vision in my mind a sense of inevitability, something that would exit from my imagination and become reality one day.

But this vision came from the bad angels. I was sure it did. What about the one the good angels had given me, where the devil did not achieve victory, and where what I said became what the whole world eventually heard: God's message to everyone that I would be the vessel of? Instead of seeing anything having to do with this in my mind, I saw my life as the devil's wife in a series of intricately detailed mental images; but when I tried to picture a world where God won and I became the prophet of his wisdom, what I saw was hazy, without detail, which made it seem less real than the vision Satan was triumphant in.

The future was a terror just up ahead, the object of my dread.

Sinister sounding laughter coming from the smoking girls standing in front of the mirrors engulfed me completely as the tardy bell rang. The sharp sound stabbed into my heart, and I felt a jolt of pain spike through my chest. I was late for class and I had no good reason for being so. I had never been tardy without an excuse. What would my teacher say? I opened the stall and hastily made my way out of the bathroom at a frantic pace, passing the smoking girls, who didn't seem to notice or care that the late bell had just rung. I made my way towards my English class in an accelerated stride, approaching what was approaching me: the immediate future, where Patrick would be.

The apocalypse was still a far-off event, but I felt as if I were approaching a mini Armageddon of sorts as I arrived at the door of my classroom. Not wanting to open it, I opened it; not wanting to go in, I went in; and it was as if I heard my teacher greet me before he greeted me, saw myself become the center of attention for a long, drawn-out moment before the kids in my class all turned their heads to look at me. I watched myself, seeing myself in my head as if watching someone else, walking across the classroom, on my way to my desk, where I saw myself sit down, awkwardly, before I'd even made my way to it. On the way to it, to my desk, I looked right where I was going, keeping my eyes locked on my destination, not allowing them to wander about the room to look at the reactions of the other students over me walking in late because, I knew, his would be one of the faces I would see looking up at me.

I felt his eyes on me, Patrick's eyes. I became overheated suddenly, as if melting under his stare. I felt beads of sweat run down my neck, and felt my forehead dampen as the skin within my tightly gripped fists moistened. And right when I got to my seat, before I sat down, dizziness came over me; I think I almost fainted. I collapsed into my seat, where I remembered to breathe, something I had forgotten to do since I'd entered the classroom. My back was aching, so I leaned over on my desk, rested the brunt of my weight on it, folded my arms on top of it, and sat my breasts down on them to ease the pain radiating from the muscles around the middle part of my spine. For a few brief seconds this pain was the only thing I was aware of until I came back to myself as my teacher's voice entered my ears.

I was in English class.

My teacher was Mr. Thomas.

He was talking about The Stranger, a book by Albert Camus that we'd just finished reading last week. He wanted to know why the protagonist didn't cry at his mother's funeral or appear to feel any remorse; he wanted to know what this said about this character. One kid, Stephen, stated the obvious, that he didn't cry because he didn't really love his mother. The teacher's reaction to this student was ambiguous, and I couldn't tell if he was skeptical of the student's response or if he agreed with it. He said, "That certainly is a possibility. Not crying over your mother's death would certainly make it seem that way, but are things in this story what they appear at first glance, or is there more to it? What do you guys think? Do you agree with Stephen?"

One girl, Erin, spoke up: "He might have just felt numb. Sometimes when I'm sad I feel nothing. I shut down."

The teacher reacted enthusiastically: "Ah, interesting, but what does nothing feel like? How can you feel nothing? Can nothing be something?"

"Yes. I think so," Erin said. "It's feeling like you don't feel anything."

"So you feel an absence of feeling," said Mr. Thomas, "but isn't this like saying you feel what you don't feel, when you say you feel no feelings...when you say you feel nothing?"

"I guess. Maybe," said Erin. "Well...I don't know. Now I'm confused."

"You're just making things more complicated," said this one kid Bill.

Ignoring this comment Mr. Thomas said to Erin: "Maybe you should be confused." Then he acknowledge Bill's comment: "Or maybe it's just real simple and like how it seems." Then he turned his back to the class and wrote on the white dry erase board at the front of the room the word "ABSURD" in all capital letters in a bright red marker. He pronounced the word out loud before he turned around and asked the class to tell him what it meant.

The class was silent for a few moments, and Mr. Thomas repeated the question: "Who can tell me what absurd means? What do you think when you hear this word? What do you say about something when you call it absurd?"

A kid named Jimmy answered, "It means like something is weird like it doesn't make any sense."

"So was the main character being absurd by not crying at his mom's funeral or feeling any sad feelings over it? Or was his situation absurd in some way?"

"Yeah. Kind of," said Jimmy, "because usually people cry when their mom dies. I know I probably would."

"So is the unexpected absurd?"

"Sometimes," said Jimmy.

"Do you think the main character expected to cry at his mother's funeral?" asked Mr. Thomas.

"I don't know. Maybe," Jimmy said.

"I think he did," said a kid named Max I knew from church. "I think he was surprised by how he reacted. I think he wanted to cry at his mom's funeral, but not for her or for himself but for the other people at the funeral so he would look normal; and not crying, not feeling bad about his mom being dead was weird, because people are supposed to cry at their mom's funeral. That's what was absurd about it, I guess."

Max was the smartest kid in the class, or I thought so. He always had something deep and philosophical to say, and what he said always seemed to be what the teacher wanted to say but was waiting for one of us to say instead. It was as if Max were his mouthpiece like the angels were God's.

"So it was absurd because it didn't make sense?" asked Mr. Thomas in a question that sounded like an answer to itself.

"Exactly," said Max.

"Why would Camus state, as he did many times during his life, that life was absurd, that the nature of existence was absurdity, as if being alive were absurd in and of itself?"

"Because it is," said Max. "We show up on Earth not knowing where we came from or how we got here or how anything did, and we're told fairy tales when were kids that are supposed to explain everything; but when we get older we realize that those fairy tales weren't true and life isn't what we thought it was, and everything becomes confusing and we realize we aren't who we thought we were; and nobody is who we think they are...and...everything becomes meaningless."

"If we're not who we think we are, then who are we?" asked Mr. Thomas, "Let's have someone else contribute. Anyone? What do you guys think?"

The room was silent. Like I said before, I was quiet but would sometimes talk up in class because I wanted a good participation grade. But on this day, I wanted to be invisible, not there, which I guess made what I did next absurd, because without telling myself to or thinking about what I was going to say in advance, my mouth opened and I said, "I think the only one who knows who we really are is God."

"That's interesting, Lisa," said Mr. Thomas. "So does that mean the self we perceive is a mirage of sorts while the person God sees is who we really are in reality?"

I nodded. "Yes. That's how I think."

"But we can't know what God thinks about us, can we?" asked Mr. Thomas.

Unless angels tell you what He thinks, I thought but didn't dare say.

Mr. Thomas continued, "So since we can't know what God knows, we walk through life not knowing who we really are while thinking we're someone we're not. Is this true? Is this what Camus means when he calls life absurd? How does this relate to The Stranger? What is a stranger?"

"Someone we don't know," said a girl named Tiffany.

"Why do you think Camus chose this title, The Stranger?" Mr. Thomas asked.

No one answered the question. Mr. Thomas paused for a few moments waiting for someone to say something, but no one did. In the absence of an answer to his question, he said, "In an essay Camus wrote on the nature of the absurd, he said there are times when we look in the mirror and see a stranger. He also said when we look at photographs of ourselves we often see someone we don't know. What do you all think of that? Have any of you had that experience where you stare in the mirror and see someone you don't recognize staring back at you? Could this be why he called this book The Stranger?" Mr. Thomas paused for a few moments then asked, "Who is the 'stranger' in the story? The main character or the people he encounters, or is it both maybe? Is the protagonist a stranger to himself? Do you think he knows who he is?"

Again no one answered. Mr. Thomas ended the complete silence by saying, "Well, I want you guys to ask yourselves this as you read tonight's chapter. And also ask yourself how the man character's life is absurd, and try to think of other examples of absurdity that you recognize in your own life." And as Mr. Thomas said all this, he was making his way to the back of the room where his desk was located. He grabbed a black videotape with no label on it from one of the desk drawers and made his way back to the front of the room. He rolled the television set that was up on a stand with little wheels beneath it to the center of the room and put the tape in, saying as he pressed play, "Now we're going to watch a short bio on Camus's life that I recorded from PBS." Then he shut off the lights.

At first, when I saw the blank black tape I thought about the video, the disgusting porno I'd seen at my baby-sitter's when I was just six.

"That's when the devil entered you," said an angel as I thought this.

Again.

And when the angel said this, it made me think about the devil once more, and this thought seemed to be the reason behind why an angel then said, "He wants you for his wife."

Again.

Something that had been said many times, said again.

This made me think about what I had thought about in the bathroom: Satan coming to me as the man I would marry, and an angel responded to this thought: "He wants you to give birth to his child."

Again.

I don't mean to make the same point over and over, but that's what the angels and demons were doing, making the same point over and over, as if they were trying to drill certain knowledge into my head through rote repetition. Is this getting on your nerves? Are you getting tired of hearing the same thing again and again?

So was I.

Right then my fear was strongest.

I tried to keep my eyes glued on the TV screen playing in front of me in the dark classroom, but they kept wanting to stray, to sneak a glance in Patrick's direction, but I didn't let them. I didn't want to see him, but my eyes for some reason wanted to look at him, and it was a constant struggle to maintain my control over them.

It was absurd. My eyes wanted to see what I did not.

I knew if I looked at him I would see him as I saw him last night in my head. I didn't want to be reminded of the awful thing I'd allowed myself to be tempted into doing, but as I thought about this reason for why I didn't want to look at Patrick, it made what happened the night before replay in my consciousness. I was damned if I did and damned if I didn't. Looking at Patrick would make me think about what we had done in my head last night while trying not to look at him caused the same thing when I thought of why I was trying not to look at him. It was something I couldn't escape. The fantasy returned. He was naked in my head again as I thought about how I had touched myself.

"Never do that again," said an angel.

Again.

"Lisa, are you a little slut?" asked a bad angel.

Again.

Had enough?

Am I annoying you? Well, I would have felt lucky to just feel annoyed by what I kept hearing and thinking over and over again. Annoyed doesn't even begin to describe it. Imagine tracing your way through those fun little mazes they hand out to kids at some family restaurants. Now imagine tracing your way through a thousand of them.

A million.

A billion.

Tracing out the same pattern again and again.

And again.

Where was the exit out of this maze? I was always on my way back to the beginning. The end was nowhere to be found. It was a lesson I kept relearning. I was learning that I couldn't control where my thoughts went. It was something I'd never thought about. I tried to send my thoughts in new directions, but they wouldn't bend to my will; their current was much too strong. I went where they went; they did not go where I went.

I felt like someone in my own head, while before I had just been someone with a head. Everywhere I went, there I was: in a place I didn't want to be, somewhere inside me.

I was locked inside myself. There was no way out.

The video on the life of Albert Camus glowed at the front of the dark classroom. I was looking up at it but not seeing what I saw. I was hearing the sounds the television made, but I did not hear what I heard. Absorbed by what was in me, I was absorbing nothing outside myself. I was in the classroom but not in it. I was somewhere else with the angels.

Until his voice brought me back.

"Look at me," I heard him say in a hushed tone.

It was Patrick's voice.

Was he talking to me?

"Lisa," I heard him whisper, "please look at me." I did what he asked me to. I glanced in his direction.

He was looking up at the TV and not at me.

He hadn't said anything. But then who had?

Was it Satan?

I wondered about this as I continued to stare at Patrick. Then, as if feeling my eyes on him, he turned to look at me. Our eyes met for a split second; then he smiled at me. I quickly looked away, wanting to blink out of existence, to become something he couldn't see. My heart began beating rapidly like it was about to burst. My chest became tight, and I had to tell myself to breathe as if this automatic function of my body had shut down and now my lungs had to be willed by me through conscious effort into doing what they usually did on their own.

A few days ago I would have done anything to get Patrick to notice me.

Anything.

A smile from him would have filled me with glee, but now it filled me with absolute terror. I still saw him smiling at me. I saw him in my head where his grin turned a shade sinister. It widened across his face, stretching upward, slicing through his cheeks, almost touching ear to ear. It began to remind me of the way I had been looking down at Tommy that day on the bus. This thought came and orbited around the Patrick I saw in my head. It joined all the other thoughts I'd thought that day that would not go away; these thoughts all whirled around his presence in my mind like rings around Saturn being thought then thought then thought again. I thought them all at once. It was as if they had been crushed together and concentrated into a single thought.

One massive thought made of thoughts.

I didn't just think it. I could see it.

It represented everything from the night before along with everything the angels had said since then mixed with all the obsessions this Monday had been consumed by. What I saw in my head didn't seem like just a fantasy or a daydream. It seemed like something alive. That's what it felt like inside my head.

Alive.

And it looked just like him: Patrick.

He was naked in my head again, still grinning at me wickedly. His face resembled a scary Halloween mask, something he could take off and put on whenever he wanted to. But the scariest thing was his cock. It extended and widened to absurd proportions. It enlarged to measure in size equal to one half his height. His image in my mind was like a glowing object in black empty space. Then everything around him changed instantly into my bedroom where I saw me in my bed wearing my pajamas. The door to my closet was open, and Patrick was standing in the doorway at the foot of my bed. He moved onto my bed. I didn't see him move inside my head. It wasn't like a movie. It was like a series of snapshots. In the next image I was completely naked, locked tightly in his grip. I was crying. Hearing me cry made him laugh. I begged him to stop, and he told me to shut up and called me a slut. He was killing me.

Killing me with his cock.

I saw this in my mind as clearly as what I was seeing out my two eyes.

I could close my eyes or look away at something else if what I was seeing with them disturbed me, but I could not look away from this. The image remained stuck where it was like a DVD still frame on pause.

"That's not Patrick, it's the devil!" shouted an angel.

The pure terror I was filled with shot up in intensity when I heard this. My perception that this presence in my mind was alive collided with what the angel said and turned into the belief that it was Satan. In a rush I remembered all the demons and angels had said about his intentions towards me, and I remembered what one angel said about the video being his gateway into my body. I felt like running from the room, but anywhere I went, I knew, I would carry him with me. How can you escape something in your head? I tried to push it out but it pushed back. It was more than a thought. It was something that made me think what I thought. That's what I perceived.

This was more than just a fantasy to me. It was a fantasy on the verge of crossing over into reality.

Everything I had thought about Patrick clashed with everything I'd thought about the devil and began to combine. I tried to separate the two, but they persisted to merge into one concept. It was as if my mind was trying to reconcile the differences between what was in it and what was outside it. That's what I think. There was the Patrick inside my head and the one outside it, and the two were at odds. It was all so alien to me. I'd always thought people were who I thought they were. The way I saw people in my mind was who I believed they were in reality. But now there was a Patrick in my head who was not Patrick. It was something that was what it wasn't.

I needed a bigger word than confusion to describe how this made me feel right then. The world mirrored the world in my thoughts, and I had always mistaken this reflection for what it reflected. It wasn't something in me, it was something I was in: the world inside my head. I had always perceived it as outside and all around me.

But now the mirror had cracked, cracked where I saw Patrick's broken image. A new variable had been added into the equation: Patrick/not Patrick. I couldn't factor it in with the rest without destroying the whole equation. All else was alienated by the presence of this paradox.

There was every thought I had ever thought then there was this thought. I wanted to reject it from my head. It was a thought too big for my brain. It didn't fit. It was leaking out my skull from my eyes, nose, and ears, gushing out my mouth, seeping from the tiny pores in my skin, exiting from anywhere the world entered my senses, expanding outward, changing the entire universe outside me, as my mind bled all over everything.

The distinction between the outside world and the one in my thoughts sharpened, the two drifted apart like polar opposites; one side contradicted the other side. My abstraction for the world no longer felt like home. I felt in the world while outside it. It was like the entire universe was splitting in two. I was on both sides of this divide, ripped in half. And I would not be whole again until Patrick was once more Patrick.

Before Patrick had been my ideal.

His image had radiated goodness into my mind. But now I couldn't look at him without thinking about the devil. I didn't know why the devil had chosen this form. It made no sense to me. What did this mean? Why Patrick?

What did the devil really look like?

I asked the angels these questions, but none of them answered me. Then I remembered what the angels had said and said and said: that's not Patrick: it's the devil; that's not Patrick: it's the devil. I thought this and thought it and thought it and thought it. And I thought about the Patrick who had smiled at me for real. What did that Patrick have to do with the one inside my head? What had his smile looked like? It was all distorted in my memory. Patrick inside my head was Satan. But who was the Patrick sitting two rows over from me?

"That's not Patrick. It's the devil!" an angel shouted again.

This left me confused. Did the angel just mean the devil was the Patrick inside my head? Or did the angel also mean the Patrick outside my head was the devil, too? Could this be true? Was the Patrick inside my head the Patrick outside my head?

Was Patrick the devil in the flesh?

As I wondered this, he continued to commit violent sex acts against me. He was wielding his massive cock like a weapon, like a sword he had me skewered upon. And right then, with this in my head, the demonic angels were saying, "Slut," constantly, without end. Saying it again and again. It was like hearing a broken record.

A skipping CD.

That was my Monday.

A skipping CD...D...D...D...D...D.

Silence and the Third Eye

I couldn't sleep. The angels would not be quiet.

It was already well past midnight, and I didn't even feel tired for some reason. It was as if the voices coming from the angels and demons were charged with a frantic energy that released in me as their words entered my ears. There was a tangled mass of anxiety moving around like electricity inside my chest, and every time I breathed in I felt the darkness of my room penetrate into my body, while inside my head Patrick was still raping me to the sound of demons chanting their mantras. I pushed against these grotesque images with invisible hands, but the fantasy wouldn't budge. I tried to picture something else instead, but the disgusting visuals sucked up all my concentration and my focus remained chained to them. The sense I'd developed earlier that what I kept seeing even with closed eyes was alive inside my head persisted through out the evening. And my belief that this "living presence" was Satan translated in my emotions into a dread-saturated terror I couldn't stop feeling.

I wanted this to end more than anything.

Sleep was where I would find relief, I believed, but sleep seemed so far away. If the angels would only just be silent for a few minutes, and if I could just stop thinking about what I was thinking about for a handful of moments, my body would eventually drift into relaxation.

Then I got an idea.

I remembered another time I couldn't sleep. I had a bad cold and was coughing nonstop, which was keeping me up. Then my mom gave me some Nyquil, and it not only made me cough less but also knocked me out about fifteen minutes or so after taking it. There was almost a whole bottle left in the medicine cabinet of the hallway bathroom. If I just took a little bit my mom would never notice. That's what I hoped.

I tiptoed to the bathroom, careful not to wake anybody. I took one capful of the awful tasting green liquid, then paused for a few seconds, in hesitation, before I drank down another capful, and then another. Taking more than the recommended dosage made me feel guilty, like I had done something wrong, but I was desperate for sleep, not so much because I was worried about being tired all the next day from lack of rest but because I wanted to be away from the angels and thought I could find sanctuary from them in my dreams.

My body is sensitive to drugs. I felt the effects after just a few minutes. The first thing I noticed was a soft numbness moving under my skin in a dull vibration as a dopey sluggishness overcame my brain. The agitated state my mind was in began to settle down. My thoughts became progressively less frenzied and began to move with a drunken slowness. The light inside my head grew dim around the obscene images, which began to ebb away from my attention as their brightness faded, while my consciousness sank increasingly into an enveloping blackness. The deeper I went into it, the farther away the angels sounded. One of them kept telling me I was a drug user. It was the last thing I remembered hearing before I disappeared into a deep sleep.

When my sleep reached its end, it was not my grandmother I heard waking me with her voice like she had the previous morning but my mother instead. She was in my dream speaking through someone else who was telling me in my dream it was time to get up. Then everything around me in the dream began to rumble in an earthquake as my mom began shaking me awake.

The light was intrusive and cruel; it stung my eyes when I opened them.

It felt like all the weight in my body was concentrated in my eyelids, and keeping them open was like bench-pressing myself. My room was a colorful blur slowly coming into focus as it stabbed my eyes. I closed them, returning to darkness, while feeling overcome with a heavy grogginess that was pushing me with all its might back down into slumber. As if from a great distance I vaguely heard my mom walk from my room into the hallway, but I knew she would return shortly. It was like a universal law, an unchanging fact: my mom would be back. I wanted to be in an alternate existence where what was true in this one wasn't true in that one.

In the darkness behind my eyes was where I wanted to stay.

The painful vision the light had brought into my eyes when I opened them was the day up ahead announcing itself to me, like an awful premonition, but it was almost nonexistent behind my closed eyelids. The nothingness I saw there comforted me with its total absence of anything, and with its complete lack of activity. But the coming day was just on the other side waiting for me. I was certain the angels and demons would be there. Thoughts about them intruded the tranquility I was within and stained the perfect nothingness with bright images of the future as I imagined it would be. I wanted to return to sleep and never leave. Not until the world became what it once was, a place where angels and demons didn't speak to me, where I was just a regular, ordinary girl and not a prophet Satan wanted to wed then impregnate with the Antichrist.

My mother returned just as I was crossing into a dream. My mom's voice grabbed me, and lifted me back up into the light, as my eyes opened involuntarily. Instantly I wanted to close them again, which I did, hoping my mom would disappear from my room. But she didn't. My mom grabbed me by the arm and pulled me out of bed, and as she did I began to collapse. She stood me up with all her strength until I began to stand on my own two feet, feeling as I did a great surge of blood rush to my head in a dizzying wave that made me feel faint. To keep from falling down, with my eyes still closed I steadied myself by resting my right arm against my mom's shoulder.

My mother said, "You seem more tired than usual. Were you up late?" The words slowly crawled up my throat as I responded, "I had trouble sleeping," and as I said this I continued to refuse to open my eyes and accept that the new day had come. My mom asked, "How come?" and I told her, "Just because I couldn't for some reason," which wasn't a lie, because "some reason" could've meant anything.

"Well, something must be up," my mom said, "because you've never had trouble sleeping before."

With just one eye open, looking at my mother, who was turning to walk out of my room, I said, "Yeah. I know."

When my mom left my room she must have been expecting me to follow her to the breakfast table, but I stayed behind for a few moments listening closely for the angels, hoping to not hear them. Into my ears came the faraway noise of the kitchen sink where someone must have been washing a dish, and outside my window a bird was chirping, but beyond that I didn't hear anything. Right then and there I said a prayer asking God to keep it this way for the rest of the day.

At breakfast I felt like laying my head down in my bowl of Cheerios and dozing off, while my sister ate her cereal across from me, sitting next to my mom who was reading the paper. I felt drugged up in a drunken daze, still half asleep. I supposed I was experiencing a hangover from the triple dose of Nyquil I'd taken the night before, and I wondered when the effects would fade. My sister had a volleyball match later in the afternoon and my mom asked her about it, and I listened while the two of them spoke, glad it was them I was hearing talk and not the angels. Then my mom asked me about what I had going on at school, and I gave her the briefest possible answer: "Nothing." She probed for more detail and I told her what my classes were going to be that day, to which she responded by asking me if I had any quizzes or tests, and I answered her no.

In the shower I let the warm water rush down my neck to my back in a soothing stream, while I leaned against the tiled wall with my head held down under the showerhead, eyes closed shut, using one arm as a pillow. I was listening to the angels not speak. It was the perfect silence. The silence was nothing, but I felt it as something; it was all around me, and with my eyes closed I saw only what there wasn't to see. Sleep still had a strong pull, and my mind had ventured back into that limbo state where consciousness edged into a dream, but there was also something else making its presence known there, a force just as strong, pulling at me from the other side, like a game of tug of war. It was necessity. The things I had to do even though I didn't want to. I was in the shower wanting to be back in bed, but I had to be in the shower because I had to get ready for school.

But still I didn't move, and I kept my eyes closed.

There was something holding me back. It was what had made me first shrink away from the daylight in terror when my eyes first opened. It was more than the drowsiness caused by the Nyquil. That played a part, but it was minimal in comparison to what really made me not want to move forward. It was something I was trying to keep out of my head, thoughts I didn't want to think. The thoughts I first began thinking the evening I committed my terrible sin.

Drifting into sleep was a step away from the thoughts I didn't want to think. I knew once I was fully awake I would start obsessing about the angels once again, along with everything they'd said to me. In my current semiconscious state, it was like I was thinking without thinking. Almost dreaming, but not quite; awake, but barely. The awake part of me was thinking about the angels and Satan, but those thoughts disintegrated when they passed into the part of me that was half-asleep near a dream. The side I was trying to stay on in my mind mirrored the silence, but its opposite was at the periphery where the thoughts I didn't want to think were edging closer in. I felt a far-off fear approaching; it was me waking up; it was the silence being invaded.

A loud banging sound at the door startled me into a state of full alertness, which was followed by my mom yelling at me to get out of the shower. In response I jumped into action finally. I began by washing my hair at a frantic pace before moving on to soap up my body, feeling a growing sense of dread as I neared the part where I washed my vagina, which I was consciously avoiding. I was afraid a demon would break the silence. I didn't want to think about that again, but as I thought about how I didn't want to think about it that's exactly what I thought. After a moment of hesitation that was disrupted by my mom banging on the door again, I washed my vagina while waiting for something demonic to make a derogatory comment. But nothing from below or above spoke to me. However, in my memory what the demon had said last time was recorded, and what was said replayed in my thoughts, where the word slut began repeating.

The word slut in my head made me think about why the demon had asked me if I was one. And that made me think about what I had done. This was something I didn't want to think about. I didn't want to think what I was thinking because I knew what I would think next. But once I thought the thought I couldn't un-think it. It was already to late to turn back the other way. I thought about Patrick. I didn't want to think about him because I knew if I did he would reappear in my mind and rape my image there like he had that night in my head, the way he'd continued to all the next day late into the night. But as soon as I thought about how I didn't want to see this in my mind, I saw it there. It was as if it were summoned by my desire not to see it.

This was why I hadn't wanted to wake up.

I knew what was waiting for me.

But that was Monday.

There was silence for now.

I thanked God right then and there for it, the silence, and asked Him a second time to let it stay for the remainder of the day. I also requested that He take the devil out of my head by making the fantasy go away. Then it occurred to me that all I had to do was stop thinking about it and it would eventually leave. But it was hard not to think about it. It seemed to draw my thoughts into it as if it were a thing with gravity that pulled everything towards itself. I tried to think in another direction with the use of sheer willpower as I climbed out of the shower and toweled off, but my thoughts kept veering off the path I was trying to lead them down like a shepherd with sheep, returning to the disgustingly vivid imagery like metal shavings to a magnet. It was the true shepherd of my thoughts. Satan was in my head, I told myself, directing all my attention at him with the force of his demonic presence and nothing else. All I had to do was stop thinking about him and he would go, but I felt like I couldn't stop thinking about him until he left my head.

I had to occupy my mind with something else.

I took a look in the mirror.

It was fogged up with warm mist from the shower, but I could still make out my reflection, although it was hazy. I could see my eyes were droopy with round lines forming deep pockets in semicircles beneath them. I looked tired. I was tired. Really tired. I would be on the bus soon, I told myself. I didn't want to take the bus to school. I didn't want to go to school. I wanted to be back in bed. I felt if I closed my eyes I would fall asleep right where I stood, but I kept them open continuing to look at myself.

There was something else about my reflection.

Something I couldn't name.

Something intangible.

I thought maybe it was just the bags under my eyes, but I couldn't decide. While I thought about it I realized the devil was not in my head anymore. The fantasy he existed within had departed with all its imagery sunk into the shadows beneath where my thoughts surfaced. But then, as soon I thought about how he was gone from my head, a disgusting image rematerialized in my mind.

I needed something new to distract me. My reflection wasn't working anymore. I was seeing the image as I stared at myself in the mirror. I had to move on. Leave the bathroom. Find something else to fill my mind with.

In my bedroom I turned on my stereo, and the radio station began to fill into the vacancy left by the angels in their silence. What I was hearing come out of the speakers was still a part of the silence to me. Every sound other than the angelic choir and demonic chanters was silence in my mind. As I heard a familiar fast food commercial come on the radio, I thought about what I wasn't hearing. What I was hearing was nothing. With the angels mute it were as if I were still asleep and dreaming.

Reality didn't feel like reality without them.

I formed a divergent path, thinking my way towards the voices coming out of the radio, trying to redirect my focus and attach it to what they were saying. I repeated the advertisements I was hearing word for word in my head while attempting to picture the faceless actors over on top of the demonic images I was trying not to see. After the last commercial played, there was a gap filled with nothing but static, and I thought I could feel the static moving through my mind, where I envisioned it as a fuzzy blackness. Then finally the morning radio program resumed with a woman's voice giving a traffic report along with a description of what the weather was expected to be like for the day before the host came on and welcomed everyone back.

That's when something weird happened.

I thought about a song I was particularly fond of at the time. It was a pop song by a male artist I'd had a long-standing crush on. In fact, the reason I was attracted to Patrick in the first place was mostly because I thought he kind of looked like him. Both their lips and eyes along with the shape of their chin and overall facial structure were similar, and Patrick wore his hair kind of like this singer did, only his was much lighter.

But anyway, the song I was thinking about came on. And when it did, mild shock bubbled up from my chest to my head where it burst into slight thoughts of surprise and wonder that were instantly subdued by as I remembered that this same thing had happened many times before.

Remembering this normalized the event and took the shock out of it, but as it became something ordinary in my mind, it did not lose its significance. It was still a mystery, and I questioned the moment and its meaning.

Had it just been a coincidence? Or had I taken a small glimpse into the future? I didn't know. What were the odds that the song would play right after I thought about it? And what about all the other times when the same thing had happened before? Were those all coincidences also? I waited for a reply from the angels, but the only voice I heard was the singer's coming from the stereo. It could have been a coincidence. Maybe. But I knew what the angels would have said right then if I was hearing them. They would tell me I was a prophet.

The angels were back in my thoughts again.

I thought of all the times they'd called me a prophet before, until my mind arrived at the memory of me in the F-Hall bathroom yesterday when I'd received the apocalyptic vision of the Antichrist's ascension to power. This recollection became what I was seeing in my head again, right there in my room, while the song continued to play, clashing discordantly with my thoughts. Its adoring words of praise were emptied of their meaning and filled with the awfulness I was feeling, as I wondered if I was seeing the future, seeing the inevitable.

I didn't want to be a prophet. I wanted the future to be open-ended and completely unknown to me. Maybe I was wrong and my vision was nothing but a fantasy. And it could have been that thinking about the song before it came on was something that just happened sometimes.

But the angels had said…

The angels. When would they be back?

I prayed to God a third time requesting that the silence remain.

Then I realized I was standing in my room naked. Just standing there, staring into space, or more accurately, staring into my mind while what was in my mind seemed to stare back at me. My towel had fallen to the floor. I looked at the clock. I only had only six minutes to catch the bus. I hadn't even picked out what I was going to wear. I still had to do my hair. I had forgotten to brush my teeth. I still had to do that. But there was no time.

I began to hurry.

I rushed into my bra and panties, then went through my closet, picking indiscriminately a black blouse and blue jeans that didn't really go well together, but I didn't think about that, I just jumped into them and took one look in the mirror, where I saw that the blouse was covered in bits of lint and cat hair that I was sure would be easily noticeable to anyone at first glance. I didn't tell you we had a cat, did I? Well, we did. A female cat named Kilgore. I loved that cat, but enough about that. Let me tell you what happened next that was even weirder than thinking about a song before it came on. I was brushing off the lint from my blouse in rapid strokes as I looked up at the clock to see how much time I had left, and as I was doing this, the song on the radio ended and the host came back on and announced the song's title, also saying who it was by: "…and that one goes out to…" Then what he said next became fuzzy, his voice garbled in static for a moment, and I couldn't quite make out what he was saying. But I thought I heard my name break through the distortion, before it cleared, just as the host said, "…from her fiancé with love."

I almost fell over.

Had I really heard what I'd heard?

I had no time to think about it, but that's all I continued to think about as I looked at the clock again and saw I had just three minutes to catch the bus (and sometimes the bus came early). I grabbed a pink scrunchie from my drawer and put my hair back in a ponytail without even thinking about how it didn't match what I was wearing. Then I sprinted from my room, down the hallway towards the bathroom, almost running over my sister along the way. She said, "God, Lisa! Watch it." I apologized, but she may not have heard me, because I was already in the living room, going past the kitchen entrance. Once in the bathroom I brushed my teeth quickly before gargling some water and spitting it out into the sink, missing a bit, which dribbled down my chin to my shirt, making a prominent wet spot there that I had no time to evaporate with the blow dryer the way I usually would. instead I ran from the bathroom, to the front door, taking a moment to turn my head to look at the great big grandfather clock in a nook in the corner of the living room, where I saw that I had less than one minute left.

As I ran from my house, the bus was just pulling up to the bus stop located in front of the house next door, and right as I reached it and was just about to step on, I realized I'd forgotten my backpack. I told the bus driver, and he said hurry up and go get it, which I did, running as fast as I could, sweating as I returned. When I climbed onto the bus my adrenaline broke down into embarrassment that seemed to be flowing into my body from the eyes of everyone looking at me. I was still out of breath when I reached my seat next to where Steph and Julie were sitting. They both greeted me, Julie smiling a knowing smile, as if she could see what I was feeling and found it amusing for some reason.

Steph asked me if I had overslept and I told her I didn't sleep enough. Then I angled my forehead against the back of the seat in front of me and closed my eyes, hearing Steph say, "You must be really tired." Julie responded sarcastically, "No, she just doesn't like us. That's why she never talks with us anymore."

I said with eyes closed shut, "That not true. I'm just really tired."

"Then sleep. I don't care. I was just joking," Julie said.

I was still thinking about what I thought I heard in my room minutes ago. Had the host really said my name? Even if he did, it could have been another Lisa he was talking about. My name was fairly common. There were multiple girls in my school who had it. But this line of reasoning was shattered as I began thinking about the odds of such a thing happening right after I'd thought about the song before it came on. One coincidence was one thing, but two coincidences right in a row was another thing completely. Then I began thinking about how the song used to always make me think about Patrick when it played, and I compounded this with how the devil always appeared as Patrick in the evil fantasy I kept having, and with what the angels and demons had said about the devil wanting to marry me. I added this all up in relation to how I thought I'd heard the radio show host say my name and how he'd then said afterwards "from her fiancé with love." But had Satan really called into a radio show to request a song for me? Where did he make the call? I mean, I knew he'd known that I would be listening right then, because he was in my head, but could he be two places at once, in my head as a fantasy, while somewhere else on the physical plane, using a flesh and bone body he was controlling from the inside to call a radio show in order to request a song then dedicate it to me by name while identifying himself as my fiancé so I would know it was him. If he could make me see something in my mind then he could also put a thought there if he wanted to. But how would I know whether it was something I thought or something he made me think? How much control did he have over my mind?

It scared me how much sense this all was making to me.

It sounded crazy but it didn't feel crazy. It felt like the truth.

And with these thoughts Satan had returned to my head again.

Thinking about him brought the fantasy back. It was the same sick imagery, and it became all I could think about. I wanted it out of my head. I had to stop thinking about it. I opened my eyes to give me something else to see, and my vision became divided, seeing one thing in my mind and another thing with my eyes. The image I was being raped in appeared translucently on the seat in front of me, as if projecting from my forehead. I almost saw it with my eyes, but not quite. It's hard to describe. It was like the image was on a clear slide layered over what I was seeing with my eyes, but not exactly like that, because it was still distinctly present in my mind, though it seemed to be on the verge of merging into the outside world and becoming something existent there, visible to my two eyes.

It was like it was becoming real.

Panic began to riot inside me. And right then I thought I heard an angel tell me to pray. But I wasn't certain. I listened again and heard nothing but the sound of the others talking to one another along with the groaning of the engine as the bus moved forward. I prayed again to God to keep the silence maintained. Then I turned to my friends and jumped into their conversation in search of a distraction that would replace what was in my mind with something else. Butting in, I said to them, "You guys are right. We never talk anymore. I want to talk."

"Then say something," Julie said.

"I just did," I told her.

"Then say whatever's on your mind," she said.

That was the last thing I wanted to talk about. I was trying to escape what was on my mind. Talking about it would just bring it closer. Or would it? Maybe it would bring relief. Maybe talking about what was in my head would release it from there somehow. But it felt like something too big to fit out my mouth. Words were just small boxes, and my thoughts felt gigantic. And even if I could express what I was experiencing, I couldn't explain in full detail the entire scope of it without revealing what I could not communicate to them without putting their souls in harm's way. The angels had warned and the demons had threatened that anyone I told about them would then be pursued by the one who was after me.

But I felt a deep need for confession.

I felt a desperate need to speak what I was feeling.

Maybe, I thought, I could open up a little without telling Steph and Julie about the angels and demons and the battle they were waging inside me, or about how Satan wanted to marry me and deposit his seed in my belly, and that he was in my head right then violating me disgustingly.

Perhaps I could tell them something if not everything.

I had to try.

I said to them both, "I want to tell you what's on my mind along with what's been going on with me, but it's really hard. I'm opening up to you right now as much as I can, but I have to be careful with what I say, or there could be, well, it sounds weird, but there could consequences, real big ones, so it's important that I watch what I say, but I want to tell you guys really bad."

"You can tell us anything," Steph said. "We're your friends."

Then Julie said, "We won't judge you. We promise. Pinky swear," and Steph nodded as if Julie were speaking for them both.

"Yes," I said, "but no. I can tell you guys a little but not a lot."

"Why can't you tell us everything?" asked Julie.

"Just trust me. I can't. I just can't," I said. "Try to see what I mean. Has there ever been anything you had to keep to yourself because it would hurt the people you love? It's like that."

"Well," said Julie, "what can you say?"

"I'm having a hard time. I have been feeling like I've been drifting apart from you two along with everybody else. I miss how we used to be. Have I seemed different lately?"

"You've been quieter. More in yourself," said Steph.

"Even more than usual," said Julie. "We've been wondering what's wrong. Just tell us. It will make you feel better. We'll be there for you no matter what. You don't have to be afraid."

"I want it to be the way it used to be. I'm in trouble. And I got this new responsibility but I don't really understand," I said, "and something bad is going to happen. I think I know what it is and I'm not sure if I can change what the future's going to be or if what I see is going to be how it is no matter what." I was looking up over their heads as I spoke; then I looked at Julie. "Am I making any sense?" I asked. I didn't wait for an answer but continued where I left off, trying to find the right words. "I have been thinking a lot of thoughts I don't want to think. It started Sunday night. Then it went on all day Monday. And it began again today. But today is different. There's something missing. I'm glad it's gone. I love how it's quiet today. But I don't know when it's going to come back. There's one thing that has stayed that won't go away, though. And I really want it to."

"What is it?" Julie asked.

"It's something in me. I can't describe it because if I do it might become something inside you, too. It won't leave me if it goes in you. I don't think so. It's like a cold. I'll still have it even if you catch it from me, and then we'll all be sick with the same germs. It's like that. Do you know what I mean?"

I glanced at them both for a moment waiting for one of them to respond. Steph had a thoughtful look in her eyes while Julie looked frustrated, her eyebrows crunched downwards towards her cheeks, all the muscles in her face tensed in expression of confusion.

I was missing my target. I tried to go deeper without bringing everything up. I reached in my mind for a thought I wanted them to think and pulled it down into what I said. "Have you ever had to be something you didn't want to be?" I said, then, thinking of God, added, "Think of your parents. What they want you to be like isn't always what you want to be like. Like, Steph, your mom makes you be on the swim team and you hate it, but you have to do it because she's in charge of you and she'll take away all your privileges if you don't do it. It's like how you have to do what God wants you to do if you want to go to heaven. What God expects you to do isn't always what you want to do. Am I making more sense?"

"A little," said Julie, "but I don't see what this has to do with the first part of what you said, which, for real, I didn't understand any of it."

"Well, what I'm trying to say is there's something I have to be I don't want to be. And there's something someone really bad wants me to become, and I don't want to be that. But there's someone that's like the best person ever on the other side of it who wants me to be another way, and I think that's how I have to be to avoid being who the bad one wants me to be, but I don't want to be what the good one wants me to be either, even though I feel I have to. But I don't even know if I can stop myself from becoming what the bad one wants me to be. There's a lot I still have to find out. Like what I was talking about. Is the future the future or can it be another way? That's what I want to know. The ones I don't like say one thing and the good ones say another, and I want to believe the good ones but I'm afraid the bad ones are right; and it's like a constant fight with me in the middle. That's as much as I can say without going to far into it. Just try to think about someone who wants you to be something you don't want to be while another person wants you to be something you feel you have to be with you in between not wanting to something else entirely."

"OK," said Julie, "like a quarter of that made sense. When my parents got divorced I had to please them both. When I'm at my dad's he expects me to be one way, but when I'm with my mom she expects me to be someone totally different. My mom tries to convince me my dad's a jerk, and my dad talks about my mom like she's the worst person on earth, but I have to please them both. Is that what you're getting at?"

"Yes," I said, relieved.

"But who are you talking about?" asked Steph.

"I can't go there," I said. "Trust me. I would if I could. But it's like what Julie said, because the two I mean were once on the same side; then they, like, got divorced, only they weren't married, but they separated, and began fighting one another." I was so absorbed in the conversation that I didn't even notice that the terrible images had left the light of my mind and had disappeared into the shadow cast by my thoughts. It was a good thing I didn't realize this because it would've come back if I had. I had to remain unaware of it being gone for it to stay gone.

As soon as I noticed it wasn't there it would reappear.

I continued to speak as the bus stopped at a red light at the turn leading to the school entrance. "Things are a certain way right now and I hope it stays that way. There's something I don't want to hear that I'm not hearing. The only problem today is I'm thinking thoughts I don't want to think that I thought yesterday and Sunday night."

Julie looked at Steph then Steph looked at Julie. They seemed to be communicating a wordless understanding towards me they both shared within a bond I was apart from. I sensed who they thought was talking to them: the abstraction of me in their heads. It was like starring into a mirror and seeing someone else, and I felt myself mutating in my mind into the person they thought was me. Then, as everyone was standing up after the bus came to a stop at the drop-off zone, I asked them both, "Have you ever thought something you didn't want to think that you couldn't stop thinking?"

Julie's response was "They have medication you can take for that, you know," and then she smiled, and said, "Just joking. But seriously, you might need to see a therapist. It might help." I knew what she was really saying. I saw through her words what she was really thinking. I was a weird person in her head.

I began to feel that way in mine.

Weird.

That's all I had communicated to them. My weirdness.

In my first class I had trouble keeping my eyes open. But I guess this was good because struggling to stay awake kept my mind focused on that instead of what I didn't want to see in my head. I was dancing at the shore of sleep where all thoughts washed away into a dream, wanting to go all the way in while my teacher's voice kept pulling me back. My eyes would shut, following a will of their own; then everything around me would seem to shout as panic would jolt me back into alertness and force me to open my eyes once more as I hoped my teacher hadn't seen me close them. This pattern continued until the end of class, and I didn't finally begin to feel fully awake until the middle of the next period.

That Nyquil stuff was strong. I told myself not to take so much next time.

As I came more and more into a growing state of wakefulness, I began thinking I was hearing the angels again, periodically. I wasn't completely sure because what I thought I heard sounded far away; however, each time I thought I might've heard something it seemed to be getting closer. But what I was afraid I was hearing was few and far between. I would think I heard something then I listen for it again and hear nothing. This pattern continued through second period the way the constant closing and reopening of my eyes repeated through first. And every time I suspected I might have heard something I would pray to God to please let me have peace for just for one day.

I had the distinct feeling that He was ignoring me.

Frequently I ruminated on the moment in my room earlier that morning when I'd thought I'd heard the radio show host say my name. I repeated the words "from her fiancé with love" in my thoughts without wanting to, and every time I did I thought about Satan and how he wanted to marry me; and when I thought about this I tried not to think it. But once I thought what I didn't want to think it was already too late. And the more I tried not to see what I didn't want to see in my mind, the more I saw it. Each time it returned, as I tried to push it from my thoughts I would begin to think I was seeing it with my eyes and not just in my mind. I would see it but not really see it. It would seem to hang in the air in front of me, suspended in empty space threatening to materialize there fully. But it wasn't like a solid object. It was see-through like a ghost.

In my mind it was Satan crossing over into reality. Not just a fantasy anymore. It was alive and wanted out of my head like a dream wanting to come true. Satan desired to replicate in the real world the imagined scenario he kept repeating in the bright, vivid images that would flash into my mind every time I thought about him. He wanted to make the fantasy into something that was actually happening for real and not just in my imagination. How did I know this? I asked myself that same question not knowing the answer until the image I was on the verge of seeing with my eyes seemed to communicate a silent understanding to me. It spoke into my intuition and peaked into the realization that I knew what the devil was planning because he let me know by putting what I was thinking in my head. Like how he made me think about the song after requesting it be played in dedication to me in expression of the love he had towards me as his fiancé. This interpretation was no longer speculation in my mind; it was a solid fact

I'm the devil's fiancée, I said in my head. Or did I?

Maybe it was Satan.

If he could put a thought in my head, I had no way of knowing for sure.

With love from her fiancé, I repeated over and over in my thoughts without knowing whether it was something I was thinking or the devil talking to me in the language of my mind. If the devil could make me think what I thought, then he had somehow hijacked my mind and taken it over. Maybe it would get progressively worse, and not only would he make me think what I was thinking but he would also move on to implant desires in my brain that would make me feel like I wanted to do something I didn't want to really, and maybe that's how he would get me to have sex with him.

I didn't know if what I was thinking was true.

I didn't know if I was thinking what I was thinking.

For a fleeting moment I wished the angels were there to guide my thoughts in the right direction but without the demons also being present to distort their message. But this feeling quickly reversed itself into gratitude that I was not hearing anything except what everyone else in the classroom was hearing, because the angels had not taught me much, that was my new opinion, and they had seemed less present than the demons since Sunday night. And if the angels were there, the demons would be also, or so I thought. But I wanted something heavenly in my head to counteract Satan's influence on what I was thinking, and to balance out the effects the horrendous imagery was having on me.

Where was God in my head?

He didn't seem to be fighting very hard for my soul.

The only thing fighting the devil in my head was myself, or so it seemed. But everyone always said God worked mysteriously. Maybe He was helping me in other ways I didn't recognize. Maybe the silence was all because of Him. Like I said, the images were not so bad without the demons heckling me about them. It could be that He was giving me a break just for one day, but if He could make me hear something one day then make me not hear it another day, then why couldn't He just pluck Satan out of my head and cast him back down into hell where he belonged?

As I wondered this, a line from the song from that morning got stuck in my head. The words were "Nobody will ever love you the way I do." In my mind the singer's voice was a faint whisper lost in the crowd of thoughts congested around the image of Satan disguised as Patrick having sex with me that I was trying not see. But as the singer continued to sing the same thing over and over, his voice began to stand out from all else and seemed to lift up from what I was thinking into almost a sound I was not quite hearing in my ears; just like how I was also on the verge of seeing with my eyes what was in my mind.

The image in my head was filled with intricate detail I could clearly make out even while trying not to see it. Satan in his Patrick form was making me suck his cock. With one hand he was keeping my head pushed down as he forced me to take him all the way into my mouth while he pinched my nostrils shut with the two fingers of his other hand. I thought I heard a demon ask me if I was a little slut, but I wasn't certain if it was just a memory from before or something I was hearing for real that came from outside my head. When I wondered this, the word slut multiplied in my thoughts and buzzed around the image like flies around a trashcan. And as I stared deeply into the image without wanting to, everything else blurred out of focus around its edges while it became clearer and much more vivid, nearing the border of visibility as all the light in the room seemed to pour forth to illuminate it. The singing voice became localized in the image and began to seem like it was coming directly from it. I looked away from it in horror, seeing it everywhere I turned my head. Then I closed my eyes and saw it still, glowing in the darkness behind my eyelids, as I put my forehead down on my desk, looking down at myself being raped.

There was no way I could escape seeing it.

It was everywhere at once.

I began to feel like I couldn't breathe. It felt like the air passageway leading to my lungs was being blocked by something lodged in my throat, and I began gagging in a reflexive attempt to dislodge it. I tried to breathe in through my nostrils, but they felt closed shut. My lungs radiated pain as they tightened in total depletion of oxygen, and my heart screamed out for air with every single beat that slammed against my ribcage. My whole chest shook frantically as every cell in my body vibrated uncontrollably into a single vibration of terror that became me. Panic was all I knew right then. It was all. It was everything. It was the universe in its totality.

All was panic without end.

My mind filled with the absolute certainty that I was about to die. The image casting its glow over my vision had stopped being just something I was seeing and had become something I was in. I couldn't breath because there was a hard cock rammed down my throat. I could feel it. And my nostrils were pinched closed by an unseen hand that I began swatting at in desperation. The fear my being was completely soaked in at that moment felt as if it was seeping out from me like liquid being squeezed from a sponge, filling the atmosphere, where it became what everyone in the classroom was breathing in. It suddenly dawned on me that they were all staring at me, all of them with the same expression on their faces that each mirrored outwardly what I was feeling within. And their faces were all in a whirl, spinning around me in a vortex I was at the center of, where everything in existence was collapsing in on me and I felt like I was looking in all directions at once as my neck pivoted my head in a vicious circle while I cried out to everyone for help with a voice only I could hear.

Then all the light in the room seemed to funnel into my eyes as a brilliant whiteness filled my mind for a single instant before all disappeared into darkness; then everything became nothing for a moment until I jolted back into existence with a loud gasp. No longer cut off from air, my lungs filled with what they had been deprived of for what had seemed like an eternity. I breathed in deep and fast, panting rapidly while feeling empty-headed and blank of emotion. Slowly I began to reawaken to my surroundings and started to feel what everyone was thinking, as if I were in all their heads at the same time, or all their heads were in mine. I became in my mind the oddity I saw reflecting back at me in their eyes . All at once spontaneously from all over the room people began asking me if I was OK. The teacher was standing next to my desk looking down at me. She told me she was sending me to the nurse. She asked me if I could walk. I nodded that I thought so without speaking a word. As she walked away from me to her desk, I heard her ask a girl named Lindsey if she would escort me to the nurse's office. Lindsey said she would.

Then a loud, booming voice that seemed like it was coming from everywhere consumed the room as it announced itself as the nurse. My teacher spoke back to the voice telling it that a student had just had some kind of episode and it looked like she couldn't breathe for a few seconds. In a delayed reaction it slowly registered in me that

I was the one she was talking about. I wanted to be something that didn't exist to anyone right then, to be invisible to everyone, including myself, as I was helped up from my desk before being guided out of the room. Everyone looked up at me, watching me go.

On the way to the nurse, the girl serving as my escort had her arm locked around mine at the elbow, making it look as if we were two little kids who were the best of friends. I was in a daze, feeling like I was walking in my sleep through a dream. I couldn't accept fully that what had just happened had happened to me. I didn't feel like me. Right then I didn't feel like anybody. It's hard to explain. It was as if a part of me had been left behind in the nothingness, and I was waiting for it to return from there without really knowing what "it" was.

What was that blank spot in my memory?

Had I fainted?

I must have. That's what happens when you can't breathe. You lose consciousness eventually. I had seen the same thing happen to people on TV all the time, only they had been drowning or were being choked to death by some attacker or something like that. Only it was Satan who'd been choking me and he hadn't done it with his hands. I tried not to think about this as we neared to the nurse's office but I was unable to stop myself, and sexual imagery began to flash dimly in my mind once more. It was not quite as intense a show as it had been minutes ago in the classroom, but while we walked I felt my chest begin to tighten again as my breathing became somewhat strained. My response was to pray to God, asking Him to make Satan go away. I repeated, "Please, God," in my thoughts over and over as my breathing got worse. I stopped walking for a moment and put my hand to my chest as I forced air into my lungs, and when I did this I felt something inside me pushing the air back the other way, forcing me to exhale when what I needed to do was inhale. Lindsey asked if I was OK and my response was "I don't know," and as I spoke I felt the air I so desperately needed leave my body. She told me to calm myself by taking a slow, deep breath and then holding it in for a few seconds before letting it out. She said that would help, she knew, that's what she told me, and right then I trusted her, even though I didn't really know her, and I followed her instructions carefully hoping she was right and it would save me. Then she reminded me that the nurse's office was only a few steps away, and I began to walk towards it with her as she gently pulled me forward.

I could still breathe, but it was as if something in me was trying to stop me from doing so. My lungs were no longer pulling air into them on their own without me making them. With all my focus turned to my breathing, I stopped thinking about what I was seeing in my head. I took in as much air as I could. I held the air in my belly for a few seconds, not wanting to let it go, and then I would finally release it in a short exhale that I would end prematurely by beginning another long inhale, which I would hold in as long as possible. I continued this in the nurse's office until I began to feel light-headed, my head was a balloon filled with helium floating high above my neck. This sensation had a soothing effect on my body, which felt much lighter, kind of like the way it feels to be in a pool, and I began to feel myself arriving at a state of calm.

The nurse was talking to another student who was complaining about an upset stomach. As I listened to the two of them speaking right next to me, their voices sounded far away, like they were coming from another room. I continued to breath in deep, and I was beginning to feel like I was all air. I was looking up at the top of the wall in front of me where it met with the ceiling when I felt a spike of pain shoot out from my heart; in response my whole body convulsed as my eyes jerked involuntarily at the nurse and the kid she was talking to. As I did this the intense sensation passed, and I returned to the weightless feeling of floating in zero gravity, noticing amid this sudden shifting of my condition that the boy with the upset stomach had a halo of light around his head for some reason. In fact, his whole body was surrounded in a luminescent, white, holy-looking glow that made him stand out from all else in the room, as if all the light in the room were attracted to him exclusively, or as if he were himself the source of the light. I studied him closely, wondering if he were some kind of angelic being but seeing nothing special about him other than his glimmer. Then his black T-shirt caught my eye and became the sole focus of my mind. I began to study it in detail with a concentration of thought I had not been able to achieve for a long time towards anything other than something having to do with the angels or Satan or something in my head I didn't want to be there.

On his shirt over its blackness was an illustration of a skinless man without a skeletal structure but with a completely exposed nervous system that formed the outline of his body from head to toe. You could also see that his brain had in the middle of it an extra eye, surrounded by a jumble of nerves shaped into a face. The brain looked to me like a parasitic alien Cyclops suctioned onto the top of the man's head, while the blue and pink lines making up the nervous system looked like tentacles coming from the brain-thing that it was using to slurp up its energy source from the host body it was feeding on. As this weird science-fictiony thought was coming to me, I noticed that above the brain written in all capital letters was the word "TOOL," which I didn't know at the time was the name of a hardcore rock band popular among the kids labeled as stoners in school.

When the nurse finally turned her attention towards me I felt like I was being pulled down from somewhere above by her voice. She asked me why I'd had trouble breathing, and I didn't know what to say. It's not like I could tell her Satan's invisible cock had been shoved down my throat at the time. If I told her that, I would have to tell her about everything else, and then the devil would come after her, too, and it would all be my fault if he took her soul down to hell with him. It was my responsibility to maintain silence towards what was really going on, but I had to tell her something, and it had to be partially true because if I told her a lie then I would be committing a sin, which was something I didn't want to do.

So I said to her that it had felt like there had been something in my throat that was keeping me from breathing. She looked at me inquisitively and asked me if a doctor had ever diagnosed me with asthma, to which I responded to by saying no. Then she asked me if I had any known allergies and I shook my head. Her next question was if I had been under any amount of stress before I'd started feeling like I couldn't breath. Bingo. She had hit on target. I was backed into a corner. I couldn't answer any other way than to say yes without telling her a fib, so that's exactly what I did, dreading what the next question would be. She asked me what had been stressing me out, and when she did I saw Satan raping me again as I stared at the floor.

"It's something I can't describe," I said to the nurse, which was true, because I couldn't, because the angels had commanded me not to.

"Are you having any boyfriend troubles, or were you feeling worried about an exam, or has anything else been troubling you lately?" she asked me.

I told her, "I've had a lot on my mind, but I don't have a boyfriend and I didn't have an exam today," and as I spoke I hoped she wouldn't ask me what had been on my mind. To my relief, she didn't, which was good, because I didn't know what I would've said back to her if she had asked. Her response was, "You might have had a panic attack" which was something I knew nothing about, but those two words panic and attack seemed to capture perfectly the experience I'd just had.

She said I might need to have a doctor look at me further, and then gave me the option of calling my mother to come pick me up or going back to class if I felt like I was able to. It hadn't occurred to me that I could go home, and I weighed the positives and negatives of having my mom come get me. It didn't really matter either way. What was in my head would be anywhere I went. I couldn't get away from it. I thought of the social awkwardness of going back to the classroom, and I thought that if I got my mom involved I would have to explain to her what had happened. Then she would ask me a bunch of questions I didn't want to answer or couldn't answer without initiating her into a world of evil.

Sensing my hesitation, the nurse suggested that I go to lunch and think about it, and if by the end of lunch I felt like going home, I could come see her again and call my mom from her office to come pick me up.

In the cafeteria sitting in my usual spot with Stephanie and Julie, I didn't tell them anything about what had just happened to me in my last class. I didn't feel hungry and was mindlessly shoveling the food from one side of my plate to the other, infrequently lifting a bite of it up into my mouth while I listened to my two friends without really hearing them. Then Julie lifted her voice to a higher octave than Stephanie's.

"Oh my God! I forgot to tell you! Guess what I heard first period? Lisa, you're going to want to hear this, too! You guys aren't going to believe this! You guys know Mary Allison, right? The senior who sleeps with like every guy?"

Stephanie said, "Yeah," and then when Julie looked at me for an answer I nodded my head barely, which she took as her cue to continue.

"Well, I heard this story about her from this girl Jessica about what she did this weekend at a party. She was at this party where everyone hated her, because she's such a slut, and they all didn't want her to be there because she doesn't have any friends, but she thinks everyone likes her because so many guys are always hitting on her because they know she's easy; and, like, she told this one girl Erica that all the other girls in the school were jealous of her; but anyways, that's what I heard from Jessica, and she told me Mary was at the party with this one guy Derrick, who she thinks she's going out with, but he was just using her for sex, and he lost his virginity to her in the bedroom of the guy whose house the party was at, and she was totally wasted, she'd been drinking vodka straight from the bottle, while being all loud and annoying everyone at the party, while everyone made fun of her behind her back without her knowing it, and she was passed out in the room after she had sex with Derrick; and then his friend Paul, you know that one football player, wanted to have sex with her, too, and Derrick said it was OK so he went in and woke her up and started making out with her, and she let him have sex with her also, even though she barely knew him and was supposedly going out with Derrick at the time, because Derrick came in before and told her he didn't mind and said he wanted her to have sex with his friend."

"Oh, my God," said Steph, "what a complete slut".

"Wait," responded Julie, "it gets worse. After Paul was done he went and told his friends and like all of them said they wanted to do it with Mary too. So they all stood in a line outside the door and took turns. There were six guys in total including Paul and Derrick. And Mary was awake the whole time. She wasn't raped or anything. She consented to every guy and said it was OK. They were all virgins except for Paul. So she took the virginity of five guys in a single night!" At that moment in the story Julie turned my way and directed what she said next at me, "Oh, and one of the guys was Patrick." Then her voice took on a sympathetic ring as she told me she was sorry. "I know you like him," she went on to say, "but he's dirty. I mean, come on! He had sex with a girl he hardly knew and it was his first time. He's a total sleaze."

"What a girl to lose your virginity to," said Steph.

"I know, right? She's a total slut. She probably has crabs or gonorrhea or herpes or something even worse than that,"

Steph said, "I hope all those guys wore a condom."

Every time the word slut had been uttered in the conversation, a graphic image of Patrick raping me stamped onto my mind. I felt what I was seeing in my head dragging me away from Stephanie and Julie, but then Julie ripped me back to the cafeteria. She asked me, "Didn't you use to go to the same baby-sitter as Mary when you were little?" and I was transported by what she said to the past. I was six years old again, sitting in front of a TV with Mary, watching the video that had introduced the concept of sex to me.

"Yes," I said to Julie, "I did"; and when I finished speaking it felt like I'd said the last word I could possibly say. What I was feeling inside devoured my voice completely, and my mind became claustrophobic with thoughts I could think but in no way communicate.

"She's such a slut," Stephanie said again. "Six guys! I can't believe it."

"Believe it," said Julie.

And there was Satan back in my head again.

I was seeing him with my third eye.

I broke down and started to cry. I tried not to but I couldn't hold it in. And as a gush of tears began rushing down my cheeks, I felt all my horrible feelings flowing away in a release of pressure that felt like an orgasm in my head. A euphoric tingle spread across my skin, leaving goose bumps in its wake. It felt so good I never wanted to stop crying. Stephanie and Julie looked at me with concern in their eyes as they both simultaneously asked me what was wrong. "I don't know how to tell you," I blubbered.

Julie asked, "Is it because of what I told you about Patrick? I'm sorry, Lisa".

"Maybe," I moaned in a voice drenched with the tears I was crying, "but I don't know. I don't know! I can't stop crying. It's other stuff, too, like, I don't know, but Patrick has been in my head all the time lately, and I don't think it's really him I'm thinking about. You guys don't understand. There's no way you can understand."

"You can tell us," Steph said in a gentle voice.

But I stood up on impulse, wiping my tears. "I've got to go home. I've been feeling bad all day," and then I left without saying another word. Julie said something, but her voice got swallowed in the sea of voices before it reached me.

Then on the way to the nurse I had an encounter I will never forget.

It was another big coincidence.

I saw Mary in the hall. What were the odds? I never saw her in school, but then right after hearing a scandalous story about her weekend escapade I just happened to bump into her. Maybe there was a reason our paths crossed. Maybe I was supposed to do something like reach out to her. That's what Jesus would have done. He would have embraced her with love. Instead I was filled with a fiery judgment at the sight of her; she seemed to glow with the hatred I felt for her right then. I remembered what an angel had said before, or perhaps it had been a demon that told me the devil had first entered me through the porno Mary had shown to me when I was six.

It was all her fault.

That's what I thought.

I watched her walk up to a group of guys and hug one of them. While her head was buried in his shoulder, the guy looked around at his friends with a look that said, "Get this girl off of me," and the others were snickering to one another, amused at their friend's predicament. The guy looked embarrassed and devoid of any affection towards Mary, who continued to remain latched onto him until he abruptly, in a sudden rush of movement that verged on violence, pushed her away and said loudly, "Look. I'm not your boyfriend. OK? I mean, you're cool and everything, but I just don't feel that way about you."

Mary turned and began walking quickly away from them towards where I was frozen in the middle of the hallway. As her back was turned, one of the guys made a coughing sound shaped into the word slut, which was followed by an explosion of laughter from all of them. The whole time my eyes were locked on Mary's face, which looked empty and without feeling; but her eyes seemed to communicate that a great sorrow existed in her beneath the surface where no one could see it. When she heard the guys laugh, she looked back at them, and as her face came back into view when she turned away from them again, I saw that she was smiling, even chuckling a little, as if she found the whole thing funny the way they did and was laughing along with them. But her eyes betrayed her actions and continued to say otherwise.

Mary continued to walk in my direction, and when I saw her looking right at me our eyes met for a brief second before I looked down at the floor and started walking again.

But Mary was heading right towards me, and as I moved to step out of her way I heard her say, "Hey." I looked up at her face of stone and her eyes that spoke to me silently.

I could have said hi back.

I could have done something.

I could of done a lot of things, but I did nothing.

All had rejected her. Her name was a symbol of shame all over school, and the abstraction of her in the heads of everyone else was the archetype for the word slut.

What was it about the way Mary was looking at me right then? She looked at me like she recognized in me something I was unaware of at the time. I had the strange thought that she knew everything I was going through, as if she saw inside my head right then with those piercing eyes of hers. I was seeing Satan again raping me in an image that seemed to be glowing over Mary's face as I looked at her, but I knew it was really in my head and not something I was seeing with my eyes.

I had the feeling she saw it, too.

I don't know why.

But I just walked away from her.

Saying nothing.

I could have done something.

Maybe I could have been her Jesus.

Maybe I could have made a small change in her life by saying just a few kind words that would've somehow made all the difference to her. But I just walked away toward the nurse's office to call my mom, feeling nothing but loathing towards her. As I felt her eyes staring into my back, it seemed that she could somehow magically feel what I was feeling, and that I could also feel what she was feeling, as if she were in me.

That's what it felt like.

Like Mary was inside me.

She walked away with me while going the other way.